UP FROM MY ABYSS

UP FROM MY ABYSS
by
BONNIE BARRIGAR

Everlasting Publishing
Yakima, Washington
USA

Up From My Abyss
by
Bonnie Barrigar

ISBN: 978-0-9983858-8-4

First Edition
Everlasting Publishing
P.O. Box 1061
Yakima, WA 98907

I dedicate this book to anyone who has fought or is still fighting the scourge of cancer. Be assured that you are not alone.

UP FROM MY ABYSS
by Bonnie Barrigar

DISASTER ONE

It was a dark and cloudy March the day I went to the doctor at the local clinic to get a regular exam and see about getting a mammogram. The last test was something I had never had done before since I had been told over and over again how painful they were. Also because I secretly wanted to depart this world which for me seemed to have nothing in store for me but more heartache. My brother, Robert, finally persuaded me to go see my personal doctor, Erick Fudd, for all these import-ant tests. I agreed because he told me how much he loved me and that we would do more things together, like hikes and fish-ing trips. These words did bring me some comfort and incen-tive even though I still felt rotten and gloomy about my life as a whole. All my life I had tried various projects in an attempt to pull myself out of my poverty and all, for one reason or an-other, failed. Still, I hung on to hopes for success as an author. At that time I had three books out on the market, all historical fiction, and was sincerely trying to sell enough of them to make a better life for myself. Even so, I was angry and discouraged over how few were selling.

"And what do I get for all my pain
Betrayed desires
And a piece of the game," shrieked out the lead singer of the rock group, The Smashing Pumpkins, as I braided my long

1

light brown hair and put on a jacket in preparation for walking the mile to my appointment with Dr. Fudd.

It was sure to drizzle that day so I'd take my umbrella too. Listening to the raucous cords of their rock tune, "The World Is A Vampire", I had turned up full blast made me feel vindicated and like I mattered.

"In spite of my rage
I'm still just a rat in a cage!"

Those lines from the continuing song made me smile maliciously. In so many ways, other people made me feel like a rat in a cage. Like one of the checkout girls at the local grocery, Stephanie Santa Anna, who always laughed at my chronic verbal awkwardness and never took anything I said or did seriously. I hoped, with a heart loaded with resentment, that someday I might find a way to turn the tables on her, force her to take me seriously. She would always laugh at the very suggestion I could ever do that. I was determined to show her though, somehow, someway, someday. In the meantime, I'd bide my time.

Besides, I had a doctor's appointment to go to. I felt the painful lumps in my left breast and hoped for the best, while dreading the worst.

As I finished getting ready for my medical rendezvous, my miniature Schnauzer dog, Pepper, left her bed and came over to me seeking love and attention with her large heavily lashed eyes. I felt a pang of love as I picked her up and cuddled with her for a few minutes. Then I put her back on the floor and gave her a treat.

"Don't worry, baby, mommy will be right back," I told her knowing guiltily that I really had no idea how long I might be away, since doctor's appointments are prone to be hurry up and wait situations.

How I hated leaving her behind, but like seemingly everything else in my life at the time, it really couldn't be helped. To salve my conscience and provide her with some entertainment in my absence, I switched on the TV. A vintage black and white version of the Perry Mason show came on. I smiled. I like this particular station, ME-TV, which shows mostly programs from the 50s and 60's. I prefer a lot of the old programs to the mindless drivel that comprises most modern TV shows. Feeling myself being drawn into the program that was meant to be company for my dog, I gave her a fond pat on her furry gray head and then left out my apartment door, umbrella and purse in hand.

Down, down the stairs I went. Finally, at the bottom of the lengthy flight, I opened the door that led out of my apartment into a dark, windy, dusty day. I felt a feeling of foreboding as I went down the front door's concrete steps and hit the sidewalk. Everything had a tinge of gray to me, even the trees that were starting to leaf-out and the crocuses in people's yards.

"Please God protect me from people's meanness and rudeness and make me behave sensibly and with tact," I prayed under my breath as I drew up the collar of my black plush jacket and sped along down the streets and sidewalks.

I hurried past the Legion Hall, then a local antique shop, then past several houses. On the walk near a local tire shop, I saw a dead bird. It appeared to be a badly decomposed dove. Seeing that added to my already intense feelings of gloom. Even so, I forced myself to continue walking briskly on. Soon I was near The Golden Arms Apartment complex, a set of apartments owned by the same insurance company that was in charge of my apartment building, Golden Sands Apartments. *Golden, yes, this small high prairie town has been truly golden to me in so many ways,"* I thought to myself with quiet gratitude. This thankfulness, though sincere could not salve the gloom I felt swallowed by that day and which seemed to permeate everything around me.

The wind was starting to really pick up and wet sprinkles were starting to appear as I passed the locally owned IGA Store. I hurried by it as I continued on my way to the clinic. I glanced painfully over to the left at a two-story, brown and tan house on North King's Street. This dwelling held a lot of memories for me both grievous and fulfilling for it was there that I spent nearly twenty years with Oscar "Ozzy" Wainwright. This man had taken me into his life and hearth when I needed a companion and benefactor the most and at a time when everyone else seemed to shun me. Even so, our relationship hadn't always gone smoothly. We had many serious disagreements, especially concerning money. Ozzy could be a regular Mr. Scrooge at times. In spite of that fault, I felt that my relationship with him had made me feel far happier and normal than I was feeling that cold spring day. At least Ozzy would hug and kiss me and make love with me now and then. He would also tell me that he loved me every day.

Ozzy's and my former home disappeared from my view as I rounded a corner at the sidewalk and I shed a tear for the love and life I used to share with him in that tall house which now belonged to a total stranger.

My tears kept falling on the sidewalk as I approached the doors of the Klickitat Family Clinic. When I opened the doors, a brisk, unseasonably cold wind blew me in. I went over to the receptionist cubicle and showed one of the ladies working there my ID. When I saw who the woman was, I felt a slight chill that was something apart from the crisp gusts outdoors. Her name was Ellen Weed and she was the sister of Kate Weed, a woman whom I had tried to set up a business with, a business which had been based on the Halloween oriented venue of gaudily decorated vehicle trunks baring candies and races by boxcars made in the shapes of coffins. It was called Ghostly Frolics Inc. and was a venture that Kate with her husband, Josh, had gone out of their way to make sure that my own participation in would be minimal. I still burned with anger toward them for making some lesser talented persons members of their board of directors, while I was left with the grunt work. Like making and placing the donation cans, sending publicity notices by fax, contacting radio stations in the area concerning Ghostly Frolics' activities, and making a coloring book related to the business.

To be sure though, I did still manage to get my revenge against the Weeds and Ghostly Frolics. I wrote a book where I was a female Grinch-like character who made a mess of Halloween and which was pointedly aimed at the Weeds and their lackeys. This bitingly satirical book was furthermore, read by me on a local radio station, to the intense mortification of Kate and Josh Weed. What's more, they and Ghostly Frolics got what they deserved. Their venture folded due to impaired business practices on their part within just a few months following their first Halloween. In the end, me and my female Grinch had the last laugh.

With great effort, I pushed these bitter memories into a shrouded corner of my mind and put on an ersatz smile and tone of voice. I showed my medical card to the detestable sister, thanked her, and then took a seat in front of a table loaded with magazines. Before picking up an issue of *Allure* which featured an article about how some movie stars were coping with chemo-induced hair loss, I pulled out a piece of paper. On it was a drawing of a Hopi Indian man weaving a colorful rug. I thought I had done rather well on the colored pencil piece of artwork. Lots of other people had praised that drawing, including my brother Robert. With a smile of slight satisfaction, I replaced it in my pocket and picked up the fashion magazine. I leafed through it in a half-interested way. The truth was I was feeling anxious about my up-and-coming exam by Dr. Fudd.

Then I found a page featuring fashions based on traditional Indian clothing designs and my feelings mellowed. In my soul I felt that this featured article tied in harmoniously somehow with the weaver man art piece in my pocket. Then my mood turned mournful and a tear fell from my eye unto the picture of the Hopi bead work leather dress I was admiring. At that same moment, I heard my name called.

"April!" called the blonde nurse who then led me to a room equipped with, as I perceived them that day, dire instruments of torture.

First, she weighed me. When I saw that I weighed more than I wanted to, my spirits crashed further down. Then she took my blood pressure and the cuff hurt as she pumped it. She followed this up by taking my temperature and then my oxygen density.

When she was done, I waited a while and then Dr. Fudd came in the room. He was a tall man with a serious demeanor and Abe Lincoln-like features.

"How has your stomach been, Ms. Berrigan?" he started off asking.

For years I had been troubled by acid reflux. But it hadn't been bothering me all that much lately and now I felt I had worse concerns.

"It's been alright. My acid reflux hasn't been bad. Actually, I feel I have a greater health concern now," I said with a tinge of dread in my voice that Dr. Fudd was quick to pick up on.

"Yes, I know. The tumors in your left breast and armpit you wanted to see me about."

"Exactly," I said wondering what might come next.

Sure enough, and without any further delay, Dr. Fudd called a nurse in and together they had me strip down to the waist and lay down on an examining table. Together, they gently felt the lumps that were especially prominent in my left breast and left armpit.

Afterword, Dr. Fudd told me that he was going to schedule for me to receive a mammogram and an ultra-sound at the hospital.

"It looks serious, but we'll have you looked over to find out how serious this is. And actually, I've seen a lot worse. So try not to worry ahead of time right now and keep in mind that even if your tests for cancer come back positive, there's a lot you can have done that will remedy it," said the doctor with a kind smile and in a tone meant to help me feel reassured. Obviously, he had seen many patients with conditions similar to mine and knowing that made me feel braver.

"That is a comfort, and I feel better just hearing you say that, doctor," I said as I slipped my black blouse back on.

Then I turned to the nurse who was a brunette in her thirties with a kind smile.

"I may have cancer and I do feel a bit scared," I told her while admiring her hospital smock which was rose colored with pink ribbons printed all over it saying "Fight The Good Fight". "But your smock makes me feel better."

"That's why I wore it. I wore it for you," she told me with compassionate honesty.

"Thanks, both of you. When you examined me you were so smooth you made me feel relaxed and like the whole thing wasn't so bad," I said, shaking her hand and then Dr. Fudd's.

Before leaving the clinic, I was given an appointment I was to go to four days later. A mammogram and ultra-sound were on the program. Despite the kindness of the doctor and the nurse in the pink smock, I walked home feeling more dismal than ever. Everything seemed dark, dingy, and even moth-eaten. Later on, I called my niece and my brother and sister-in-law and they were all supportive and sympathetic.

That night, I walked my dog and went about my evening tasks with a sense of dread. Already, I was starting to feel like my getting myself checked out for possible cancer might be an awful mistake. What the hell did I have to live for anyway! After bedding down with Pepper, who felt for my pain and sympathized with me in every way she could show it, I cried myself to sleep. That night I had a dream I had had before and which was to be a reoccurring one. In it, I heard an infant softly crying. In response, I sat up on my bed and saw a cradle nearby. Going over to it, I saw a baby less than a week old laying in there wriggling in the cradle's pillowy softness and wearing a blue jumper. I knew that the boychild was mine as he had my features and hair color. Feeling motherly love and eager to nurse him, I picked the child up. But at that moment, I received a terrible shock. My flesh and blood baby turned into a cold lifeless doll. I screamed in shock and anguish. Then my "baby" disintegrated in my arms like a rubber doll that had decayed with age and fell at my feet, a pile of arms, legs, and other lifeless parts. Understandably, I burst into tears, then my dream mercifully ended.

This dream always made me wake up feeling rotten. I knew what it meant, it was an allegory for my strong emotional pain

8

over never having birthed a child. In reality and in this horrible world where a woman's reproductive system has a cruelly short shelf-life, I was past the age of childbirth. I wanted to die because it had taken me this long to become mentally and emotionally stable enough to raise a family and now I happened to be chronologically and biologically "too old". I will never forgive nature and life for this horrible outcome. No earthly reward could ever make up for this horrific and heart-crunching loss. I wanted to hurry up and die so that I could go and be reborn in a world where there was no such thing as menopause. Since nobody would have understood this momentous pain, I secretly prayed for death.

The next few days leading up to my mammogram were dark and windy. The day of my mammogram was the darkest and windiest of all. It was even spitting a cold rain outside. As I walked to the hospital dried ugly brown leaves twirled in circles on the sidewalk. They reminded me of the dryness and ugliness of my own life and the fact that I felt I was spinning around in a circle I couldn't get out of. Still, I put on my bravest face and checked in with the receptionist. Thank God, Ellen Weed wasn't there. I waited with my eyes too full of tears for me to be able to take the least interest in any of the magazines littering the table like so much literary trash. In a few minutes, I was called into the mammogram lab. I dried my tears and braced myself for the worst, having remembered so many horror stories about how painful a mammogram was supposed to be.

Sure enough, the dreaded device squeezed my breasts, first one and then the other, between some metal panels. Still, the technician was gentle and the whole deal was not nearly as painful as I expected it to be. In retrospect I thought that it wasn't anywhere near as painful to get a mammogram as some women had complained it was. I found myself almost wishing that I hadn't listened to them and had taken breast exams on a routine basis. The young lady technician even got me to take part in a raffle to win a new food blender. When she was done, I thanked her and then went to the part of the lab where I would be given the ultra-sound exam. To my pleasure, the woman giving the ultra-sound was Asian. I have always liked Asians and feel a special kinship with them regarding their customs and culture. This lady was very gentle too and I noticed that she had on a purple T-shirt with glittery, colorful butterflies printed on it. It reminded me of a shirt I had made for myself that was a darker purple with a whole flock of butterflies I had drawn myself. I had made several copies of this butterfly festooned shirt and sold them at a local consignment store. The ultra-sound technician had me lay down and be examined with her ultra-sound wand and some sticky stuff I found highly unpleasant. Still, she put me at ease by telling me about the butterfly houses she had visited all across the country. In fact, it was at such a place of winged wonders that she bought the T-shirt she was wearing.

When she was done, I told her a cordial goodbye hoping I might see her again soon. Then I went to the receptionist's desk where I was told that I would be contacted as soon as the results were in. I thanked them and started for home. It was pouring cold rain. Inside, I was pouring bitter tears. I made it home and then walked my dog. I had made a little raincoat for her and she enjoyed wearing it, especially on a late afternoon like that. Luckily, she finished her business before it started thundering and thunder it did. Like a big cannon explosion.

After the walk, I called my brother.

"April, it really pains me that you have cancer. I wish that there was a way I could take it on myself for you," he said in a tone that was sweet and sincere.

We talked for half an hour while the thunder raged outside. Inside little Pepper was shivering and clinging to my side. Robert explained that his own Miniature Schnauzer, Henry, was doing the same. Both of us laughed and gave each other our love. I spent the rest of the phone call talking with his wife, Cindy. We talked for awhile about breasts and cancer. Her own mother had gotten a really bad case of it and had *shudder* lost both of hers. But she had lived long and well afterwards. We also talked about a dress I was making.

"Sweetie, I would love it if you made a dress for me. I'll pay you for the labor and material," Cindy had suggested knowing how sewing was one of those activities that could put me in a positive mood, at least for the brief time I was embroiled in it.

"I'd be glad to, Cindy," I said wondering how I would find the time with all my other activities.

At the present time I was also writing. Inspired by my Irish heritage, I was working on a historical novel based in Ireland during the time the Irish were fighting to drive out the Vikings. I always worried about not having enough time, but always seemed to manage to. Me and my sister-in-law gave each other our love and then during a thunderclap that sounded like it could have split my apartment roof in half, told each other good-bye for now.

I spent the rest of the evening crying and drawing pictures of black butterflies with skull-shaped images on their wings. I even made a few examples of them out of wire and sheer black nylon. I had Goth friends who would love those morbid faux insects and buy them from me. How I hated being alone. Even with my family to talk with on the phone I still felt very alone and like I was being forced to face this potentially deadly disease all on my own. Sure, people were praying for me, but this brought me scant comfort. Like being out in the rain sleeping under a blanket made of black butterfly wings. That night I dreamed that a whole swarm of black butterflies came and bore me away to a world where there was no menopause and where a youthful Cambodian man held me in his arms as I slept.

The next morning, I got up with my 5:00 alarm. Even though I hate to wake up early, I have to because of Pepper. This is the result of my dog getting older and thus unable to hold her pee and poop well.

Getting up so early was especially hard on me now that I possibly had cancer, but I bore it with patience born of love and knowing that I needed her love now more then ever. So I fed her, put on face lotion, dressed adequately, and took her out for her morning walk. This walk always led from my apartment through the lawn at the local funeral home. Looking at the stark white building and the weeping willows that stood near it, I thought with morbid satisfaction that I might be buried there soon. I almost wished that I could be although because of Pepper I half-assed wanted to keep on living.

After the walk, I placed her back on my bed and fell asleep for the next few hours before 7:30. During this brief spell I had a peculiar dream that did give me a few good feelings. In it, I was at the Pearly Gates of Heaven where St. Peter told me to pay my admittance to "that great land in the sky". In response, I gave him a glass jar with three of my malignant tumors floating in it.

"Thank you, April. Now enter in the realm of the blessed," said the bearded and berobed old fellow.

"Thank you, my good man. And thanks to my tumors I am now rid of the World and it's dire ugliness, hopefully forever," after saying that, I flew into the heavenly clouds although I didn't grow wings. I appeared able to fly well without such superfluous appendages.

12

Then my 7:30 alarm stirred me awake. I leaned over and hugged Pepper and then was on my feet. My next morning project was to go to the local gym called "Exercise Galore!" I really didn't feel up to it, but I forced myself to go for a work-out because I knew it was good for me. Besides, I was obliged to keep myself in shape.

Though still feeling tired, I got myself together and hurried down to the gym. I looked in the door and saw that Mutt and Kandy Gasserbury were on duty that day. That was bad.

"Oh no, not the cleaners!" I said under my breath as I stuck my membership card in the door. I was quoting a dwarf character in David Bowie's "Labyrinth" movie who said that remark in reference to an abominable diesel-driven machine that cleaned out the tunnels he happened to be walking through.

To me the quote fit since the obnoxious Gasserbury's were real fanatics about keeping the gym tidy. In fact, they acted an-noyed by me being there to work-out when they wanted to mop the floors and scrub down the gym equipment. Both of them affected phony "Veddy British" accents and manners and Kan-dy, the blonde vinegaroon, had been very short with me ever since I got into an argument with Mutt because he had been eager to dish out advice to me regarding the way I was lifting bar bells. It was advice and criticism I hadn't asked for and my reaction was "Hey, you're not the boss of me!" But Mutt was an oversized bulldog of a man who wanted to run everyone's life.

But what really had turned the sour old blonde against me was *Blood In The Xekong River,* a book I had written about Laos during World War Two which she had deemed to be too "full of violence, sex, and heavy drinking to be fit to read". Actually it wasn't and I had in fact written it to show a balanced view of both sides of the war. Still the woman had made up her ugly little mind.

I put on a brave face and checked in. I even said "Hello!" to Mrs. Gasserbury who turned her back to me before replying. Mutt didn't even reply when I greeted him. With courage and determination, I put my best effort into my work out and got through it. How I wished that I could have instead been working out at The Steel Horse Gym which stood up on the mountain grade. I was now barred forever from that better quality gym because the owner, Velarie Kaine, was a mean, narrow-minded person who had objected when I had a meltdown and was, by her standards, a piddling drama queen. As I saw it, Mrs. Kaine objected to other people putting on dramas simply because her enormous ego couldn't handle someone else being the center of attention, if only for a moment. Also, she took offense to some remarks I made at the time, remarks that she interpreted to be threats of suicide but which actually weren't. All my life, I've had problems saying what I'm trying to say and cruel, close-minded people like Mrs. Kaine have always interpreted the worst about me.

As I walked home from Exercise Galore!, I was crying bitterly over my exile from The Steel Horse Gym. It was nippy and windy. The wind blew a dented beer can at my feet. In despair and anger, I kicked the can as though it was Mrs. Kaine's robust old head. Like mental hornets the words of her friends, who I thought were my friends too, stung my mind as they took her side saying snidely, "Well, what did you expect, April? Your suicide talk scared the hell of her because she had people in her own family that died by their own hands! Shame on you!" I truly believe that those people's coming down on me so hard and with such dire misinterpretation of my words, coupled with the gym mistress' harsh and petty rejection of me from her gym were factors that made my cancer worse than it would have been otherwise. With renewed force, I kicked her tin can head into a nearby bush thinking with burning resentment about how Mrs. Kaine made me want to die of my cancer.

14

I was feeling really down by the time I trudged up the stairs to my second-floor apartment. I opened the door and there was Pepper wagging her stub of a tail and smiling at me. Seeing her made me smile in spite of myself and forget the steel-hearted gym instructor for a few moments. Wanting to walk her before the threatened rain started pouring down, I hooked her up to her leash and took her bouncing down the stairs and then out the door of my apartment building. As I came with her down the sidewalk to the lawn outside the funeral home, where she did her business, I thought of my own possible death and felt angry and sad, actually more sad than angry.

I had taken my dog out in the nick of time because as soon as we came back in the apartment complex, it started to rain a real gusher, with lighting and thunder thrown in for added excitement. Right then and there, Pepper started shivering and brushed against my legs with her soft furry little body.

"It's all right, Pepper love, mommy's here," I said softly as I picked her up and cuddled her until she stopped quivering.

In moments, we were up the stairs and in my apartment again. I was hungry, so I got to work on making myself some breakfast. It would be an apple, a poached egg, and toast with jam that day and I would count every calorie.

As Pepper settled down in her little sleeping basket with a bone-shaped treat, I thought of my tumors and felt oddly comforted. I had heard of how cancer, if left alone to run its own course, would cause a person to lose weight rapidly. Thinking that way made me feel like maybe I should just not take whatever treatment was offered to save my life. Better dead and thin with a full head of hair than surviving, bald, and fat! Months ago I had decided that I wanted to die and go be reborn on a planet where a person could eat whatever they wanted to and how much they wanted to and their bodies would oblige them by converting whatever they ate to energy rather than fat. I had made a promise to Robert and Cindy that I would get myself checked out for possible cancer. But that morning, as I dined on my spare breakfast with the wind blowing the rain around and rattling my balcony windows in a hectic gale, I wondered if it was a promise worth keeping.

I spent the rest of the day working on a dress and a doll, both of which I would attempt to sell at the Aimee's Attic Consignment Store. I hoped that it wouldn't be raining the day I brought those items to that street corner shop. When I was done, I spent the rest of the day sitting on my sofa and holding Pepper while I cried my heart out.

That evening it was my brother who called me.

"So how did your exam go, lil'sis?" he asked. I could hear Henry panting in the background. Pepper was panting too. It was a bit of a frosty night with a lot of humidity. That happened whenever the fog settled down about the area like a tight, shivery, white shroud.

"They did a mammogram and an ultra-sound, beloved brother of mine," I replied. "And the first wasn't as painful as I heard it was."

"That's good. I was hoping everything would go well for you. But you probably won't see the results until a few days, maybe a week, from now."

"I guess that's the way it works, Robby."

"Well, try not to worry about it and we'll be praying for you."

"Thank you. I appreciate every prayer. So, how is the work you're doing on your truck coming along?"

"It's coming along fine. The steer shift needed some work. How are you doing on your dress? The one with the turtle-shaped buttons you've been working on."

"The dress is coming together fine and I enjoyed making the buttons myself."

"Good for you, you're so creative."

"You're creative too, Robby. The way you like to rebuild vehicles from scratch."

"Ha ha. It's just what I like to do. But our sister, Delane, was the most creative of all."

"Yes, I know. I learned everything I know about sewing from her."

"She was also an award-winning cake decorator."

"I'll never forget her sugary masterpieces. Like that cake replica of the tower in Balboa Park she completed just a few months before she died of cancer."

"She didn't, *sob,* have to die like that. But she refused to get medical treatment because she wanted to cure herself with herbs and vitamins instead."

"I will never make that mistake, dear brother."

"I know you won't, lil'sis. I know you won't."

We finished our phone call and then I went to bed for an uneasy sleep. That night I cried myself to sleep again and had another dream about my broken doll "baby". I also dreamed about my breast tumors. If it came to that, I was reluctant about the idea of having them removed to save my life. Perhaps my life wasn't worth saving in spite of the promise I had given my brother. After all, why should I continue to live if the world deemed me too old to take part in the things that made up a meaningful life – like marriage and family? During my youth, I had been cursed with no luck in that direction. When it came to growing a family, every man I came in contact with either couldn't or wouldn't!

Thoughts of these betrayed desires of mine tormented me as I roused from sleep to a dull feeling of consciousness. I got myself out of bed and held Pepper tight. This physical bonding with my beloved pooch helped chase away the clouds of misery from my mind enough for me to get my morning going. I fed her and gave her water. Then I dressed and took her out. There was an early spring damp in the air and it was cloudy, but thank God it wasn't raining. I took her in the direction opposite to the way I usually went with her. I dodged the funeral home lawn this trip and instead took the sidewalk leading past the white Presby House Museum. Built by a local Attorney named Winthrop B. Presby in 1902, this Victorian-style white mansion with tall pillars, lofty gables, and a gray tiled roof is one of Goldendale's finest historical attractions. This distinction is well-deserved since each of its 22 rooms hold authentic antiques and are set up as they were when the building was new.

As my dog and I strolled past it, I thought with fond sadness of how Ozzy liked to go with me and look over this fine old house. He was especially fond of the old time coffee grinder display situated in a small nook upstairs. Many of these grinders were over a hundred years old. Several were wooden with curving metal handles and drawers you could open to retrieve the coffee from once it was fully ground up. I have such a coffee machine in my apartment, an inheritance from my antiquities collecting mother, Maxine.

Pepper and quickly distanced ourselves from the old building with its golden crocuses and sprouting green lawn. After all, we didn't want to linger anywhere since it just might rain any minute. I cursed my foggy brain for not advising me to dress myself and Pepper in the proper rain gear before starting out. We hurried past houses and several minutes later, turned a corner by a tall barn. This led us down a road into Ekone Park. We went along a paved road until we reached a grassy field near the town's rushing Little Klickitat River. Pepper and I then picked a trail leading further into the forest there. The leaves were just starting to come out on the trees and there were a few catkins budding on some of the willow trees. Aside from the gurgling of the brook nearby, all was silence.

After continuing on along the trail, I noticed something most out of the ordinary. Looking down on the path which was a bit muddy and twig-strewn, I saw what my limited knowledge of animal foot prints told me had to be those left by an actual wolf.

"But there aren't any wolves in this part of Washington State," I blurted out loud to Pepper who was sniffing the large canine paw prints with gusto.

Not knowing what might come next, I picked her up, feeling a touch of apprehension mixed with a touch of curiosity. This last feeling was enhanced when I glanced to the side of the path and saw a large gray boulder. On it were unmistakably the words "Be brave". To add to the unreal seeming effect, this sentence looked like it had been scratched on rather then written with a pen or pencil.
I shrugged my shoulders and placed Pepper back on the ground. We walked from the path to a paved road that led past the local pool and what used to be my and Ozzy's house. No one was there, but I looked over at the upstairs windows and for a moment thought I saw him waving at us from one of them. Whether that was his phantasm or just my imagination,

I can't to this day say for sure. Whichever it was, the vision brought me comfort.

It was also a great comfort that my dog and I made it home that early spring morning before the rain started.

DISASTER TWO

My life continued on its dreary way for the rest of early March. It was simply a blur of gym work-outs, sympathy cards and phone calls that brought only cold comfort, and my sewing and writing. Sometimes, I went to church, but I had long ago embraced the concept of God only wanting me to survive but not thrive. Indeed, that seemed to be the fate Heaven had dictated to be mine. Perhaps in another world happiness and fulfillment would truly be mine. A world that wasn't quite so harsh and limiting and full of robot people with robot ideas. My only true joy was my dog. I guess I wanted to keep on living for her sake.

Then came March 15th and an ominous phone call.

"April, the results of all your tests are in and you are to see Dr. Fudd about them," said the smooth-voiced receptionist on the other end.

Hearing that made me feel a bit queasy and apprehensive, but the part of me that wanted to live for Pepper, for my brother, and for the chance to see my books sell, helped me hold together.

"Okay, when can I see my doctor?" I asked, trying not to let my voice sound as shaky as I was feeling at the moment.

"Dr. Fudd can see you at 12 pm on March 19th. Would that

21

work for you, April?" replied the receptionist.

"That would work out fine for me."

"Good, I'll have you slated for 12 noon on March 19th."

"Thank you. I'll be there."

"Bye now and be brave."

"Bye."

As I hung up the phone, I noticed Pepper wiggling at my feet. She understood. I picked her up and cried softly into her fur.

I spent the next few days leading up to March 19th feeling as though I was in a living nightmare. Even so, during these cloud-shrouded, dark days leading up to my foreboding medical appointment I did manage to accomplish some worthwhile projects, though my heart wasn't at all in them. I did finish a dress I was working on, a powder-blue shift for spring with white turtle-shaped buttons that added to the effect. A woman on a visit from the nearby town of White Salmon bought it and gladly paid my forty dollar price. Earlier I had finished the dress I was making for Cindy and she paid me twenty dollars for it. Because she was family I charged her twenty dollars less than I normally would have. What's more, a neighbor down the street read a copy of the first chapter of my Irish historical fiction book, and being of Irish derivation himself, insisted that I sell him a copy when it first came out. I was still working on the doll. I was embroidering tulips and daffodils on its dress, so finishing it was taking a bit longer then the dresses. But though I often felt tired and depressed as I labored over the tiny stitches, I was still determined to do my best job on it. No matter how rotten or defeated I happen to be feeling at the time, I never give up on a project until it is done to my satisfaction.

Pepper too helped keep my spirits up with her frequent walks and face-licking charms.

I even went to my part-time jobs and applied my best to them. The first one was doing a shift as a docent, or guide, at the local Golden Gallery where several local artists, including myself, had featured art items. I had five paintings and three of my dolls on display there. It was basically my job to welcome people and show them around the exhibits. Another employee had charge of the cash register in case a sculpture or some other item sold. Sometimes my pictures and dolls sold. Nothing sold that week, an outcome that added to my cloudy-minded vista. Still, I put on a cheerful face and did my curator's duty. As Marilyn Manson had sung in his creepy, but knowing way in his tune "Dope Hat", "Everywhere I go, the children love the show, but they fail to see the anguish in my eyes." It always bothered me that people never could see the anguish in my own eyes. On the other hand, the small amount of money I received from working at the Gallery was a comfort, albeit a cold one.

I also continued on with my job working as a domestic for Mr. Peterson who lived out in the country and was seventy going on eighty years old. Every other week, I did his laundry, sweeping, scrubbing, and whatever else he needed for a scant sum of money. Still, it was earnings I was grateful for, even though I've always hated doing housework with a passion. I wanted to die over the fact that I was doing this drudge work instead of pulling in money from my books. Even so, Mr. Peterson was a kindly old widower who was pleasant to visit with between chores and that made the whole ordeal a little easier, but not by much.

In the meanwhile, time continued to burgeon forward towards the dreaded 19th like some relentless locomotive. What added to my misery was that my anxiety over that approaching day was preventing me from sleeping well. Finally, the dread day arrived and with a cold dark sky threatening rain. I put on pink wellingtons with yellow flowers around the top edge and made the best of it. To match the rain boots, I was wearing a pink dress and had my hair tied back with pink ribbons. Putting on a rose-colored raincoat, I was out the door and down the stairs.

As I hurried on my way to the clinic, the damp wind stung and bit me. Biting and stinging me worse were my conflicting ideas about the possible gravity of my condition. If my cancer turned out to be fatal, I didn't truly want to die unless I could be sure that there was an afterlife better than this one to go to. Unfortunately, I could never quite believe, enough to ease all of my fears, that when I died I would find eternal bliss. I might just go into nothingness. No feelings, no thoughts, no nothing. On the other hand, I was half sure that I didn't want to continue to live if it meant having a life where I had to walk to everything, no matter how sick I might happen to be. It wouldn't have been so bad if I wasn't enmeshed in a situation where I had no one to rely on for rides, or for anything else for that matter.

Just at that moment, I walked past a brown house with a yard full of tulips bobbing in the breeze. I looked up from the flowers and there was a little brown and white Schnauzer bouncing on the back of a sofa behind a large window. I thought then of Pepper and knew that I wanted to live. I had to.

I turned a corner and then followed the sidewalk up to the clinic. I came in the door and checked in with the receptionist. Thank God the awful Ellen Weed was not on duty. With a forced smile I showed all of my medical cards and my ID to the receptionist who appeared to be a genuine Yakama Indian lady and then took a seat by the magazine table. But instead of picking up one I leaned back, closed my eyes, and prayed.

"Thy will be done, Thy will be done", I said uneasily under my breath.

I seemed to have been kept waiting for the time it took to build the pyramids of Mexico, then a nurse with red hair called my name. I followed her into a small room where she subjected me to the usual battery of tortures. The worst was the weigh in. In spite of my best efforts, I had actually gained two pounds that week. *Boo hoo!* All the time I was thinking, *why do they have to put a person through this routine checking of the vitals if all they are going to be doing that day is talking with their doc?*

When the nurse was done, I was told to stay in that room and wait. I smiled as she left the room. I helped myself to a drink of water with a small paper cup from the room's sink and then settled in reading a copy of *Woman's Day*. It did feature some nice pizza recipes.

Time passed and then in came Dr. Fudd, his dark, homely face looking more serious than usual. In his hand was a box of Kleenex. It was obvious that he expected me to go completely to pieces. But I wasn't going to. By his side was a nurse with a kindly smile. I said "hello" to her and she said "hello" back.

"Ms. Berrigan, I have some news that will be jarring, but I will help you deal with it. I know what a strong girl you are from past examinations and now you need to lean on that strength. You see, the results of all your tests show you tested positive for breast cancer," Dr. Fudd said with a forced smile as he handed me the box of tissues.

"But.... nobody told me to get breast cancer," I blurted out, trying to use facetious humor to drown out my own angst. I wasn't stunned or dismayed. Even so, part of me, the part that wanted to live for Pepper, for my brother, and to, hopefully, see my books sell, was saddened and disappointed.

I took a hankie, but refused the rest of the box. He set it aside and continued on with the "bad news."

"I'm sorry. Nobody tells anybody to get cancer. Cancer doesn't discriminate. It just happens."

"Thank you for telling me. I had to know, doctor."

"Your tumors are cancerous, but try to keep hopeful. Just how serious they are and what stage they're at, I can't say right now. Even so, the treatments they have these days are nothing short of miracles."

"I know. I'll fight this thing with everything I've got!"

"Good for you, Ms. Berrigan, and I'm going to check you into Shaxu Cancer Center in The Dalles. They'll know how to treat you."

"Thank you. I will report to Shaxu and do whatever else I need to do in order to win against this thing. I will fight this thing wearing pink ribbons!" I told him adamantly.

From then on the phrase "wearing pink ribbons" would mean that I was in this cancer battle to win.

"I'm wearing pink ribbons too!" said the nurse, who had been silent the whole time, as she pointed to a pink breast cancer awareness pin on her pants pocket in a spirit of camaraderie.

Dr. Fudd ended the appointment by telling me that I had every reason to be optimistic. That made me feel vastly relieved and stronger. Also on the plus side, his nurse had made me feel vindicated and like I had someone on my side after all.

That night I dreamed again about my baby that morphed into a doll, and this vision of disappointment filled me with the usual feelings of grief and foreboding. I woke up and felt a great surge of acid rushing up through my esophagus to my mouth.

It was burning and tasted like bile. Most unpleasant. I had eaten late that evening so I had nobody but myself to blame for this vile upsurge.

While my darling Pepper slept soundly through it all, I mixed up a concoction of soda in water and drank it. To further combat the burning in my throat I sucked on a cough drop. I followed that with some soda crackers and a glass of milk. Feeling vastly better I sat up and read "The Magician's Nephew" by C. S. Lewis. A half hour later, my stomach had settled down to normal and I went back to bed. It was one o'clock in the morning, but such late night stomach upheavals were almost routine for me.

With my acid stomach under control, I went back to sleep and was soon having a much pleasanter dream. In it, I was walking the pebble-strewn shore of the Columbia River and came upon a cluster of empty white clam shells. Among them was a whole, closed shell as white and as pure as could be. I opened it expecting to find a pink clam inside. I thought of my neighbor Andy who told me that he often found pearls, albeit less than perfect ones, in the oysters he would find on the Columbia's river bank. Andy always made me smile. So did what I found in the sealed shell. It was not a mollusk creature, but a note on white parchment which read, "HEALING".

"A good omen if ever there was one," I said out loud while thinking of the cancer hospital which my doctor was sending me to and which had the ironic name of Shaxu. This is ironic because sháxu, pronounced as "shahoo," is the word in the Yakama Indian Language for "clam shell".

Refreshed by this dream that had taken such a positive turn, I awoke the next morning feeling like I really was going to confront this cancer and, with modern medicine on my side, possibly win. In spite of my late night stomach eruption, I felt full of energy and ready to take on the day. I fed and walked Pepper while admiring the salmon-pink sunrise. After I returned to my apartment, I got ready to go for my gym workout. While there, I breezed through my routine of arm curls, benching, and bar bell lifting. Thankfully, The Gasserburys were not on duty that day.

After returning home, I had breakfast and then took Pepper for another walk. It was a calm day with the sun just starting to shine through the clouds and fresh grass coming up in every yard. I heard robin calls now and then.

When I was done with my walk and back in the cozy confines of my apartment, I got a phone call that made my day even better.

"Iil' sis, I would like to take you out on a hiking trail in the Simcoes. You, me, and the dogs could spend all day up in those hills," invited my brother.

"I would love to go on a hiking trip there. When will you be over to pick us up?" I asked full of joy at the prospect of joining Robert for a walk up in that nearby mountain range.

I would be sure to bring my camera as the area was abundant with impressive lakes and brooks along with every kind of indigenous wild life. We might even see a bear or elk up that high.

"I'll be over at 1:30, so you and Pepper be ready to go," said my brother cheerfully.

"We'll be down there, beloved brother of mine. I wouldn't want to miss an outing like this for anything. Will Cindy be coming too?" I asked.

"Of course, she loves being in the outdoors. She has gardening she wants to do, but that can wait. She even packed a lunch for us."

"I'll bring something to eat too. Love you, Robbie."

"Love you too, lil'sis. See you at 1:30."

"See you and Cindy at 1:30 too."

"Will Henry be coming?"

"Of course. We couldn't leave him out of this adventure."

When Robert and I said our "goodbyes", it was only 10:00. I spent the rest of the morning writing on my Irish book, *The Battle For Galway*. I also baked some apple turnovers. When 1:30 rolled around, I got a call from my brother and met him and Cindy down in my apartment's back parking lot. Besides bringing Pepper and my camera, I also had the turnovers in a large plastic container. We would have a grand picnic in the woods indeed.

All that day, we walked about on the still frosty mountain trails. We saw wild flowers just coming up and heard birds in the trees nesting. Deer were everywhere - as were hoards of chipmunks and squirrels which were just coming out of hibernation. But our greatest surprise came as we reached the very top of those lofty hills. On a ledge right across a small canyon gap stood what was unmis- takably a wolf. He didn't come near where we and our dogs were and a second later had loped off into some cave or rocky crevice. I did manage to take his picture though..

"That's peculiar. Wolves don't usually come around these parts," remarked my brother.

"I think that animal was a sign of some kind, an omen," I said as I showed the image of the elusive, lordly animal to my brother and sister-in-law on my digital camera.

Both of them were stunned and amazed.

"What kind of omen, April?" asked Cindy, as she wrapped her red and white scarf tighter around her neck against the cool wind that was starting to pick up.

"I don't know, I just have a good feeling about it," I replied as I put my camera back in the pocket of my pink plush jacket.

"I have a good feeling that we should start a campfire and sit around it telling stories," interjected my brother.

"Great idea!" I agreed.

"Yes, we need a family campfire get-together," said Cindy.

So, as dusk began to settle over the Simcoes, all three of us gathered pieces of wood and put them into a pile. When it was big enough, we lit it and made a roaring bonfire. In minutes we were warming our toes and recounting tales of adventures in the woods we had enjoyed in times past. As we humans talked, our dogs crowded around us almost protectively – watching, waiting, and listening. Hours passed and soon the woods and sky were as black as the eyes of a bear, which for all we knew might be close by observing us. My brother then decided it was time for us to leave and go back to Goldendale.

Gathering up the dogs, my brother, sister-in-law, and I made it back down the mountain trail and got into my brother's car. Just before I got in with Pepper, I heard a howl off in the distance.

"Hey, that's a wolf," I said in awe.

"Probably the same one we saw earlier," said Cindy as she and Henry got in the front seat beside of Robert.

What a grand family outing we had that day, full to the brim with happy memories and back woodsy magic!

DISASTER THREE

From the day of March 19th forward I wore pink in some form or other. My family became more lovingly supportive. They started taking me to all of the places I needed to go, whether a grocery stop or doctor appointment. It was if knowing they could lose me to cancer sobered them up and forced them to see that I needed their help now and then. I had tried learning to drive throughout the years, but failed at each attempt because of an impaired body reflex condition.

As a further show of love and support, my niece, Katie, started wearing pink ribbons. Although I hadn't been aware of it, she had always thought highly of me. Every book I ever wrote she bought and read with zeal. Then she'd tell everyone how great it was and that they should buy a copy. Through her recommendations, I sold quite a few of my novels.

It was just as well. I needed all of the support I could come by. From March 19th on through what remained of the month I was to be subjected to a battering of tests. Four days later, I reported into the local hospital again for some more ultra-sound exams. The Asian technician gooped up both my breasts and armpits again and then ran her magic wands over and around me. Sure enough, the lumps were still there and bigger and more painful than ever. Still, her manner was sweet, gentle, and reassuring. Asians have always set my heart at ease during the direst and most testing of times. I noticed that she was wearing another butterfly T-shirt. This one was a black one with a glittery pink monarch made of sequins and rhinestones festooned across it. She told me that she had put it on herself in her spare time.

"You did a marvelous job. I love it," I told her as her wand continued to slide over my bare flesh.

"Thank you. You say that you have sewn together T-shirts like this and decorated them. You are quite an artist yourself," said the lady with an accent that carried a sweet touch of Korean.

"Oh, I don't know how good an artist I am but I try my darnedest. And I was thinking. Why don't they set up a butterfly house here? I think it would do the town good."

"Every town needs one. But it would take some money and organizing."

"I'm sure it would and it would be worthwhile."

I then listened with intense interest as the lady told me about some of the more exotic butterfly houses she had seen all over the land. Maybe if I sold enough books, I could have one built.

At the end of the exam, however, my anxious feelings about the tumors returned on black dusty wings. It hadn't helped that someone in the office had told me I might be getting "a new set of twins", meaning my breasts might be removed and then rebuilt. I didn't like the idea even though Medicare would pay for it and the sort of reconstruction that was possible was nearly flawless. Still, if loss came to loss, I would prefer sticking cotton in my bra and having them work on my neck and stomach instead. As I saw it, nobody would be seeing my breasts, except in the most superficial way and everyone could see my turkey wattle and pot that persisted in spite of all my best exercise and dieting efforts. But Medicare wouldn't pay for neck or stomach slimming surgery. Damn it all to hell! Feeling anxious about the possibility of surgery, I voiced my fears to the butterfly-loving technician.

"If I need surgery, I hope I can get a lumpectomy. I really hope I can avoid needing a mastectomy," I said nervously.

"Try not to worry about that right now, April. I understand why you're afraid, but I can tell you're a strong person who could handle anything in order to get better. With the right chemo treatment, you might not even need surgery. So, try not to bother your mind with that now. Think of butterflies instead," as the fine lady said this, she laid her hand on my shoulder in a way that felt like a butterfly settling there.

"Thank you, ma'am, I will dwell on butterflies and pink ribbons," I rejoined, starting to feel better and not so afraid.

"Yes, and pink ribbons. Wear them with pride," she added with an encouraging smile.

"I will, ma'am, I will," I promised as I stood up, rebuttoned my blouse, and prepared to leave.

As the Korean ultra-sound technician and I exchanged warm "farewells", my artistic mind began to be filled with ideas for making designs that incorporated both butterflies and pink ribbons. I was starting to feel better and more optimistic. Then I stepped outside the clinic door into a down pour of rain. This put me back in a gloomy mood.

I walked home in the rain, my mood becoming more depressed and defeated with every step. Soon I was wading across puddles of water that were growing wider by the second. It was a relief when I made it back to the safety and warmth of my apartment with my little gray and white Schnauzer. She welcomed me at the door and when I picked her up, she chased all the gloom away. I changed into drier clothes, grabbed a pink umbrella, and took her out for a short walk. The rain puddles had flowed together, making small pools by then. But we didn't mind. We were both wearing raincoats. Still it was chilly.

After our walk, I spent the rest of the day cleaning my floors, giving Pepper a thorough brush out, and doing a chapter in my Irish book. Later that evening I watched Babylon 5, a science fiction serial which features an alien race that deems complete baldness in women as the major feature of beauty. I was wondering if the medical treatments I'd soon be taking might make me a candidate for joining a colony of those space aliens, called Centauri, who are human enough in appearance and have a rich aristocratic culture. I was already trying to figure out ways to get wigs, but deep down inside I wished I had the courage to just get my head shaved and wear a band of golden thread and sequins after the fashion of a high-class Centauri lady.

But though my family was largely supportive at this time, there were a few others who weren't. In fact, I happened to have a few enemies. One of the worst of them was Lucy Smites, a pudgy blonde who had made up her mind to despise me for the pettiest of reasons.

All full of herself and feeling that she was second-to-none in her exercise of the "social graces", Mrs. Smites loathed me heartily because of the social clumsiness born of my disability. She felt I had insulted her sons George and Ralph, because I often got loopy in the head and said the wrong things at the right time and vise versa. Often, when people spoke to me, I was slow to respond due to mental fogginess. Sometimes, I neglected to answer them at all. Mrs. Smites interpreted it all as deliberate rudeness and made me a target. Behind my back, she sneered at me giving me the label of "The Mad Hat Lady". Mrs. Smites slapped me with that nickname just because I frequently wore hats in all seasons. I did this as much as a way of hiding myself as shading myself from the sun and wind. Sadly, no cap or fedora could conceal me from this spiteful woman's ire and sarcasm.

I guess it was fortunate that in the beginning I didn't even notice her targeting me, so lost in my mental fog was I. Then some so-called friends made the dire mistake of drawing her rancor against me to my attention.

"She hates you because you're socially awkward and female. Really, she hates all females," said one man who I thought should have kept such ideas to himself.

Really, he should have. What made the situation worse was that so many idiots seemed to be afraid of Lucy Smites.

"Oh, you don't want to get on the bad side of her. She's mean and malicious," they all told me in a way that just made me angry – at them.

Because whenever someone sets me up as a target of their hated for no particularly good reason, I set out to deliberately give them a reason. In response, I doctored up a picture that Mrs. Smites had circulating on facebook, so that I was center stage in it, crashing her party. When she objected to it loudly, I sent her another picture. This one was a truly sinister drawing I did that depicted me as a female phantom of the opera causing a massive chandelier to fall on the audience of an opera house, as did Lon Chaney in his version of the silent horror classic.

"If you don't like the pretty one I did of myself. Well, how do you like this one!" I told her defiantly by text.

In response, she threatened to sue me or get me arrested. I stood my ground.

"You can't scare me. You can't hurt me," I texted her back. Then I unfriended her.

With my cancer already starting to eat away at me, I didn't care if she tried to kill me. In fact, part of me wanted her too. I was defiantly ready. But she backed down. Aside from rumors about her talking trash about me, which people should have kept to themselves, I heard nothing more about her. My party-crashing picture remains defiantly on my face book page.

My appointment with the ultra-sound lady was my first in a series that became progressively more dismal and unpleasant. On the 26th I was to go to The Dalles for some blood work at MCMC at 8:30 am. No, they couldn't do it in Goldendale, because they didn't have the equipment at the hospital. I faced what I had to do like a trooper. I got my brother and sister-in-law to drive me to the clinic in The Dalles, Oregon and left Pepper in the care of Andy Day, a kind neighbor who loves dogs. In fact, he has an adorable little chihuahua named "Skippy". It was a perfect arrangement. I would pay Andy for "puppy sitting", while Skippy and Pepper always loved playing together. As it was, we even joked together about our two dogs being boyfriend and girlfriend. It was all in harmless fun, however. Both of them had been fixed so there was no danger of a puppy aftermath.

Secure in knowing that my dog would be in the best of hands, I got up at 5:00 am, my usual time, and handed her over to Andy. Then at 6:30 am I boarded my brother's car for my blood work (bloody) appointment in The Dalles. As I rode there, I apologized profusely to Robert and Cindy for their having to do this for me and for their having to get up so early in order to take me to my medical destination. They both assured me that it was okay and that they didn't mind doing it for me.

"We just want you to get better, lil'sis, 'cause you're family and we love you," said Robert as he turned to favor me with a sincere smile. I was sitting in the back seat stewing in my anxieties.

After fording the distance past several miles of dry hills grooved by terraces made by grazing cattle, we were finally across the bridge between Washington and Oregon. Below us, on the rocks in the rolling Columbia River were flocks of seagulls. Ozzy always said that whenever there were seagulls roosting on the boulders near the shore it was a sign that there was a bad storm out at sea. I didn't doubt that one could be brewing. The river waves were wild enough and the sky above them was gun-metal gray. Even so, an even fiercer storm was raging inside me.

We arrived at the MCMC (Mid-Columbia Medical Clinic) and I put on my sweetest face and checked in. I was handed some papers to make out and then we waited for several minutes that rolled into half an hour. Finally, my name was called and a nurse with Mexican features and a strong Spanish accent checked my blood pressure, weight, and heart beat. Afterwards, she led me to a room where two women waited for me with needles, tubes, and vials – all for taking my blood samples. I said "hello" and then sat down, preparing to get poked and determined not to show that I noticed or cared. What I wasn't prepared for was what happened next. For over fifteen minutes, the two medical technicians poked and prodded me, but couldn't find a vein they deemed worth using. When I, at the limit of my patience, insisted that they keep trying, they ended the session and insisted I go home. They told me they couldn't use any of my veins, because I was badly dehydrated. I learned a valuable lesson that day. I learned that in order for my veins to be plumped out enough to be used I had to drink plenty of water. In retrospect, I curse my slow, dull mind for not realizing that I probably could have told them to wait for a couple hours while I downed eight glasses of water, then have the blood drawn. But I couldn't think that far, so the whole twenty-mile trip had wound up being pointless. I was scheduled to come back three days later.

Robert and Cindy were good sports about it and told me that it was all right, they weren't mad at me. But from then on, I noticed that my brother's car was practically stocked to over-flowing with bottles of pure water whenever he took me on a medical trip.

That night I cried myself to sleep and woke up the next morning feeling like a fool for having started this program to treat my cancer. In the wee hours of morning, it all hardly seemed worth the trouble. Then kisses on my hand from Pepper and a phone call from Robert telling me how much he loved me, assured me that it was. All was well, and he'd take me back to the clinic on the 29th.

7:00 on the 29th rolled around like an emotional wrecking ball, but I was prepared. That morning I got up extra early, fed and walked Pepper extra early, handed her over to Andy and Skippy extra early, and then loaded up on pure water until I felt I was sure to drown. My brother's car arrived and I climbed in, still feeling half-asleep. We were just out of the driveway of my apartment complex when my phone rang. On the other end, was the most aggravating news from the desk girl at the clinic I was supposed to report to that day.

"Ms. Berrigan," she announced flatly. "we can't take you at the clinic today because the materials for testing your blood haven't come in. We'll have to reschedule."

"For what day?" I asked starting to come awake.

"I don't know yet. I will call you when the materials arrive. Then we can schedule an appointment."

"Remember, I have to come all the way from Goldendale."

"Yes, we know and sorry for any inconvenience."
"Thank you. I'll tell my ride then. We were just on our way to you."

"Bye."

"Bye."

I sheepishly told me brother what had happened and he drove back to my apartment's parking lot.

"At least they didn't phone you when we were halfway to The Dalles already," said my brother with surprisingly good-natured humor. I had to agree with him.

Two days later I was told to report back to the same clinic on April 1th at 9:30 for the blood draw and tests. When the day arrived, my brother took me to my appointment. My sister-in-law wasn't along. She had to help babysit a sick grand-daughter. As I rode along, I downed every bottle of water in my brother's vehicle, so by the time I got to my appointment my insides were sloshing like the waves of the Columbia River which happened to be really rough that day. I thought of all the times I had rode with Ozzy on that broad band of water in his little motor boat when it's waves were calmer and the days were sunnier. How I wished he could have been with me that moment to hold my hand and help me through this ordeal. The day was April Fools Day, and I failed to see any humor in the occasion.

It was raining as my brother parked his car and he followed me into the clinic. I checked in and then we waited. He occupied himself on his smart phone, getting messages from family and looking up items on the internet. All of the people that contacted him said "hello" to me and wished me good luck and good health.

"Say, April, this is really interesting about the ice caves near Trout Lake. I've been to them and you told me you've seen them too," he said as he showed me a picture of some of the pictographs in one of the old caverns.

I nodded my head and smiled thinking of all the times Ozzy and I went on outings to those ice caves. They were fascinating. I enjoyed the ancient Indian cave art on the stone cavern walls and noted that they were icy cold – even when the temperatures outside were up in the three digits.

Soon a nurse, a black lady this time, called me into the medical chamber of horrors. Although her manner was kind enough, the disappointment of being told my weight and the binding of the blood pressure cuff were worse that day than ever. Then she led me to the place of the worst pain of all – the room where the two technicians waited to draw my blood! I put on my sweetest grin and sweetest voice and hoped they would be able to take my blood with ease this time. They sanitized the area near my elbow and then ran the needle in. It slid in like bat teeth going into a ripe piece of fruit. I was to have no trouble that day. The two women took several samples and put them into five different tubes. I chatted with them banally the whole time about my dog, where they lived, and what pets they had. One of the girls confessed to being a "horse person". I had to suppress a laugh. Indeed, with her long face and mane-like coif of blonde hair, she did almost look like her favored animal. She confessed to owning a stable of five. I told her that I sometimes liked to go riding horses at my nephew's ranch. As the horse-faced technician and her partner took the last sample, I wondered drearily if I was going to be able to take part in that fun activity once my treatments began.

After the appointment, my brother took me out for a meal at Vientiane House, a Laotian restaurant. I loved the food there, especially the larb, which is a spicy, marinated meat dish, but had been reluctant to return after my first meal in that fine eating establishment with its paintings of Laotian landscapes and display of dolls in traditional silk dresses. That time I had gone there with Ozzy and things were a lot happier for me then. That was years before the health crisis which was now blighting my life. I was hoping that the next time I dined at the place I would be financially better off. It was my cherished ambition to make a lot of money, at least enough to get off SSI and Social Security with my books and then go have a meal at Vientiane House to celebrate. Instead, I was having a pity meal under the sword of a cancer diagnosis. Still, I made the best of it. I dined on a serving of larb along with some fruit salad and flirted with Akamu, the exceedingly handsome owner of the eatery. My brother talked with him about fishing, both locally and in the Mekong River which flowed near the village where Akamu was born.

That night, after walking Pepper through the maze of mud puddles, I talked with two of my nieces on the phone, telling them of my whole experience and asking them how they were doing. Both of them were fine, but had been worried about me. I told them my trip to the clinic had gone better this time and they told me that I just needed to keep on with the program. They both had faith things would get better for me.

"But maybe they might get worse for awhile before they do get better," I told Katie sardonically.

"I know, but you're as tough as turkey feathers and the medical treatments aren't as harsh and are better than they used to be.

Back in the day, people taking chemo would feel like the treatment was worse than the disease after the first infusion, what with all of the nausea and tiredness. So I'll keep praying for you and try not to worry," she told me with cheerful optimism, tinged by a touch of reality.

That night I dreamed I was standing in the rain. It was so dark I didn't know at first where I was. Then a stroke of lightening flashed and I saw two things that didn't really shock me, but touched my heart with a tinge of sadness. I saw a headstone with my name on it and a freshly dug grave. In despair and grief, I threw myself into it as the downpour continued to drench my hair and long black gown. In the distance, I heard the mournful whistle of a train. *Could it be the Long Black Train, that iron clad collector of souls, coming for mine?*, I wondered as I slowly slipped into unconsciousness. "The Long Black Train", a country tune by Josh Turner, happened to have been one of Ozzy's very favorites. In my dream vision the "train" of that song's lyrics was taking me to be with him.

I awoke the next morning and went about my activities, feeling more like an automaton than a vibrant human. Pepper and my family were the only bright spots in days that seemed the color of a damp, dark, gray dishrag. Still, I sold a doll. I also worked on a spring blouse for myself. The cloth it was made of was a soft pink floral print polyester.

My birthday on the 7th came and went bringing me more sorrow than joy. I did get a card or two from people who remembered and treated myself to a chocolate sundae at the town's Dairy Queen, but aside from these small gestures, the event was over all dismal and empty. Emblematic of my life as a whole. It didn't help matters that my brother belonged to a religious sect that frowned on observing birthdays as something close to sacrilegious. For years I had secretly regretted ever being born in the first place. Now I was starting to feel that same regret again because everything about my life seemed too pointless.

Five days later, I was to be subjected to more exams. These were to be an MRI and a PET scan and I needed to have both of them done in Portland. I wanted to cry. I thought of all the happy times I had spent with Ozzy in Portland when he went to the Veteran's Hospital in that fine city. No matter what other people may say about it and no matter how crowded it has gotten now with tramps and addicts camping along the side of every road and in every park, to me Portland will always be the place where Ozzy and I enjoyed touring the city and the flower-dazzled countryside around it. I loved the museums and the parks where we would walk our dogs during the years when both of us raised Miniature Schnauzers. Now I would be spending all of my time in Portland being crammed in two foreboding machines. A time of all torture and no pleasure awaited me. The place I was headed for was called *Epic Imaging* and had been especially set up with various devises for taking internal pictures related to diagnosing cancer cases. It really helped that Cindy was able come along for my moral support too.

Dreading it all and feeling close to tears, I put on my best false face and false manners and checked in. All the time I filled out the papers a desk girl gave me and then waited to be summoned, the words of the song, "Masquerade" from Andrew Lloyd Webber's *Phantom of the Opera,* rang through my mind's ear.

"Masquerade! Paper faces on parade!
Masquerade! Hide your face so the world will never find you!"

Yes, I would do my utmost to hide my tears and fears, no matter what tortures medical science had in store for me. It didn't help my uneasiness that Epic Imaging was such a newly established business that the whole building was still being worked on. Shelves were still being set up and a door was waiting to be put in place. Here and there walls were in need of paint jobs. I looked around me and sighed hoping that the equipment I was going to be put through was in more serviceable shape. I was directed to slip into a changing cubicle and put on a medical robe, while Cindy waited for me in a seating area nearby. After I put my clothes and other items in a locker in that seating area, a technician directed me to a room with a forbidding hazmat sign on its door. I shuddered, but kept my composure. They would do the MRI or Magnetic Resonance Imaging device first. This would take half an hour, *ugh*. First, the technicians put contrasting solutions in my veins. Then they gave me some ear plugs, saying the machine would be intolerably noisy, and had me lay down as I was rolled through a long bright tube that seemed endless. I closed my eyes, afraid to look. What I did see as I was first put into the device reminded me of that scene in the latest movie version of *It* where a young boy is swallowed head first by an evil clown-like creature. The last thing he sees is the gullet of the monstrous clown which seems to be ringed with bright lights. Thankfully, this monster eventually released me intact.

Then the technicians had me lay on my stomach with both my breasts sticking through a couple of holes in the machine's conveyor belt and I went through again for another scary loud ride. This took another thirty minutes. When this ordeal was done, I slipped back into my hospital robe and was led to another room with a hazmat sign with Cindy holding my hand. She took a seat while I was led over to the PET scan machine. To my irritation, I was given another round of intravenous fluids and then put through the machine. It was smaller, less noisy, and all I needed to do was lay back and be rolled through a donut-shaped device. Somehow, it reminded me of the Stargate in the *Stargate* television series where time and space travelers use a donutlike device to go instantly to different worlds. I commented to the technician about how the PET machine reminded me of a stargate and she agreed on the semblance. I also found that she was a fan of that sci-fi series which put me vastly at ease and made my journey through it a lot more bearable. It also helped that the whole trip only took fifteen minutes and did not involve me lying on my stomach. For someone like me with chronic acid reflux, lying in that position can be real torture.

After all procedures were done, my brother took me and Cindy to a Chinese restaurant where I ate a big meal. I was understandably very hungry. To prepare for the two scans, I had to go without eating and could only drink lots of pure water.

I went home in a bit of a better mood. I took Pepper for a long walk and then spent the rest of the evening holding her while watching an episode of *Stargate* and then *Babylon 5*. Later that night, I made a drawing of myself dressed as one of those bald Centauri babes.

That coming Thursday, I had an appointment to see Dr. Jane Katskill at MCMC for a follow up. I didn't like it. I was to go to work for Mr. Peterson that day. He was a very kind old fellow, however, and said that he would be just as happy to have me clean for him the following Friday. On Thursday, I left Pepper with Andy and Skippy and got in my brother's car for The Dalles clinic. Cindy couldn't come with us. She had a bad cold. The waves along the Columbia were being dashed so high that day I wondered if they might start creeping up on the highway. But they didn't and we got to MCMC on time though buffeted the whole way by a cold violent wind.

After I checked in, Dr. Katskill welcomed us in her office warmly. She was about forty and slim with long black hair. Her manner was professional though tempered with a touch of caring as she gave me the results of my tests. I had tumors in both my breasts and armpits as well. Plus a spot on my liver and in my shoulder muscle. Yes, the cancer had spread.

"You will need chemo therapy. What will be required after that will be determined after you've done the chemo for awhile," she informed me in a way that was firm, but concerned.

"Okay. At least it sounds like it's treatable," I said, trying to sound strong.

"Oh, it is if you do everything the doctors at Shaxu tell you to do," she added.

"So how long does it look like my little sister is likely to live, doctor," asked my brother seriously.

"She could have years to live. But it all depends on how well she responds to treatment," said Dr. Katskill.

"That's good to hear," I said a bit confused by all of the medical jargon she'd given me during the talk, but still trying to be hopeful over the words *she could have years to live.*

These words had made my brother smile, looking hopeful too and relieved. Then Dr. Katskill continued.

"One more thing, April. You may want me to put a port in before your treatments at Shaxu can begin," she said matter-of-factly.

"What's a port and why do I need one?" I asked politely, but with aspartame sweetness.

"A port, which is also called a central intravenous port, is recommended for you because it just makes it easier for staff to take blood samples and give intravenous fluids. It's also easier on you because it will save you from being poked so much," said Dr. Katskill with a patient smile.

I frowned at her. I don't like to have gadgets placed in me unless my very survival depends on it, like, for example, a pace maker. I certainly don't like gizmos put in me for convenience sake. For me, ease, convenience, and even comfort are beside every point. Still, I was willing to hear Dr. Katskill out and get as much information about that particular gizmo as I could. Unfortunately, my brother seemed already sold on the issue.

"And if I don't have one put in, can I take my medicine by intravenous methods instead, without a port?" my inquiring mind wanted to know.

"You can, but I wouldn't recommend it."

"Why, doctor?"

"Because some people find the fluids used irritating to the veins. Chemo can be corrosive."

"That bad, huh? Well, what if I decide not to have a port put in at this time? What if I wait until I actually see burning and corrosion serious enough to ensure that I can't take the fluids except by a port?"

"We could try it that way and a person like you who has healthy veins to start with might not even have those kind of complications."

"Remember what happened to Delane," interjected my brother in a way that was totally inappropriate.

He was implying that I had to go along with everything these doctors suggested or face dying of cancer the way she did. Couldn't he see that I wasn't objecting to taking the treatment? I just felt I should have some say in how I'd be taking it. So I ignored him. But because of everything that was being thrown at me, I was starting to feel ambivalent and confused.

48

"April," continued the lady doctor, who was really trying hard not to sound pushy. "I can put the port in for you on April 25th. Would that work for you?"

I told her "okay", but still had my doubts. I might just call later and cancel that operation. I liked the idea of having a port embedded in my flesh even less when I read that the operation required my lying on my back with my head lower than the rest of my body. Another torture position for a person with acid reflux.

Dr. Katskill continued with her lecture.

"You will have constipation. This will come from the pills you will be taking to combat the nausea caused by the chemo. But there are ways to deal with that. People who eat plenty of prunes and drink prune juice don't usually have any problems."

At that point, I felt like saying "No thanks to the anti-nausea medication. I'll take my chances with whatever nausea comes my way." As I saw it, it couldn't be any worse than the vomiting spells I often got at night because of my acid reflux." But I kept that idea to myself.

"I'll just take enemas," I said instead blandly. The doctor shook her head.

"I don't like to see any of my patients take enemas unless their lives depend on it because they can become addicted to them. You see, when people use enemas all the time, their bowels get used to that as a crutch and before long they aren't able to have bowel movements naturally. What's more, with chemo patients there is the possibility, no matter how slim, that they could poke themselves and get an infection. That can get nasty," she said calmly making a point that while it was valid was just not interesting to me.

"She got the idea of enemas from her mother who was into a lot of alternative medicine fads and ideas," Robert interjected in way that was as annoying as it was malapropos.

I ignored him and made up my mind that when it came to giving myself enemas, I would use a "let's and say we didn't" attitude. If I was careful I wasn't likely to poke myself and get infection. Still, was I going to have to worry about every little sore or hang nail I might get during chemo?

"That Dr. Katskill sure is nice," said my brother to me as we left her office after the appointment and climbed on board his car.

"She is," I replied as I got in the seat beside him. I liked the woman enough but didn't agree with everything she had recommended.

I was glad though that she hadn't been pushy with me. I have always preferred doctors who aren't.

In the days leading up to the 25th, I asked a lot of people a lot of questions about the pros and cons of having a port installed. I read a lot too, both in books and on the internet. Some people were in favor of the device, some were against it. I was determined to make up my own mind about it. Finally, my niece Katie helped me make up my mind once and for all.

"It seems to me that port would need cleaning at the part that attaches to the intravenous wire. You might have to clean it yourself or have a nurse come in and clean it for you," she suggested.

That turned me off big time. If I had to worry about keeping any part of that gizmo clean, it was a complication I felt I could do without. God knows, I didn't feel up to taking on any more cleaning chores of any kind. It was taxing enough then to just have to worry about doing the routine duties involved in keeping myself, my dog, and my apartment passably tidy.

"That sounds like a chore I can hardly be bothered with now. I'm tempted to just forget the whole deal. I still might want to have a port installed though if it means that less medicine would be circulating throughout my whole body. A port might make the fluids more localized than if they were given intravenously. Could it work that way?" I suggested.

"It might, but I'd check to make sure," Katie cautioned.

"I'll do just that. Thank you," I said, feeling more determined and like I was getting back control of my life, even if it was to a very small degree.

Bolstered by confidence from talking with my caring and wise niece, I phoned the Shaxu Cancer Center and asked a volley of questions related to ports and the need for them. I talked with an on-duty nurse practitioner named Anne Lynne Poule and learned that yes, I would be required to keep the device clean at all times and that however the chemo was put in me, it would still permeate my whole body just the same.

"But, you really should have the port put in. It would just make it easier for the staff...and for you," she added as though that consideration of me was an afterthought.

I was not impressed and had already made up my mind that for me such a gadget would be redundant. I could just see the thing paining me and feeling like a lump under my saddle as I did my benching and squats.

"If you don't have the port put in, that could mess up your

schedule for getting chemo treatments altogether," Nurse Poule mentioned as a last word of caution.

I didn't believe that and her saying that didn't make a bit of sense to me. So pretending I hadn't heard that last part, I thanked her for her time and then hung up. Minutes later, I phoned MCMC and told them to cancel my appointment to have the port installment surgery.

"I have decided not to have a port put in unless my life depends on it," I said to the desk girl. Then Dr. Katskill came on and I gave her the news.

"Well, if you ever change your mind and decide to have the port put in, I'll do it for you!" she told me with respectful tolerance. I stood my ground, but was nice about it.

"Thank you, doctor. I will cross that bridge if I ever come to it," I told her calmly, but firmly.

Then I wished her "good day" and hung up. I felt freer and more at ease. Like I had dodged some kind of bullet.

Two days later, I had an appointment at MCMC for something else. I was to get my heart checked to make sure it was strong enough to tolerate my taking the medicines I was scheduled to receive – one chemo and two biologics. The latter were an antibody and a hormone blocker. Antibodies, which are meant to destroy the pathways of a cancer's growth are sometimes hard on a person's heart. My brother and sister-in-law took me to the clinic and waited while I was put on a heart monitor. I was deeply relieved and grateful to learn from the exam that my heart was in good shape and capable of tolerating the medicine.

I dreaded heart disease because I knew that treatment for it would bring a limited diet which for me would be worse than the cancer itself. That outcome reminded me of a joke I once heard on a comedy record my sister had.

First comedian, "I'm going to keep my heart healthy and live a long time because I've given up cake, ice cream, potato chips, and pizza."

Second comedian, "Why on earth would you want to live?"

That grim prospect would not be my fate and I would be receiving my first chemo treatment on April 30th, May Eve, the day Wiccans have for eons deemed to be their witch festival.

While the last days of April still lingered, it was turning out to be not such a cruel month after all. On the 29th it was an unseasonably mild day and the waters of the Columbia River were calm – almost mirror-like. So, Robert got the urge to take me out for a fishing trip on a boat that Ozzy had willed him. He came by it this way. In the early spring months before my beloved passed on, he made out a will of sorts. It wasn't complete, that is, it didn't name heirs for all of his possessions, but at my insistence, it did name my brother as the receiver of his boat and me as the receiver of his dog, Checkers, and $10,000 in cash, if anything should happen to him. I got Ozzy to do this, because although he remained strong at seventy-eight, he did have a serious heart condition.

After Ozzy died suddenly that dreaded day of May 24th, there was a beautiful funeral for him at a Pentecostal Church we often went to together. Afterwards, he was cremated and most of his ashes were taken by his sister, Annabelle, who buried them in a family graveyard outside of Vancouver, Washington. I took enough to fill a heart-shaped locket that I wear to this day. I also got the money, which was little comfort to me though it did help pay some expenses. I also got his dog, who in spite of the tender care and love I was glad to give her, just wasted away. That led to my further sorrow. Thank God, I still had Pepper who had tried to befriend the little black and gray Schnauzer. Of course, Robert got the motorboat.

Ozzy had been happy to will it to him since they were both good friends who had many an adventure together. My man especially liked going up with Robert in his small yellow private plane. They flew all over the State of Washington in it and often I went with them.

My brother had also gone on fishing jaunts with me and Ozzy on the Columbia River. Now it was five years since Ozzy's passing and Robert was helping me relive the joy of those experiences in the April of 2019. As an added bonus, he had invited my neighbor, Andy, to come along too. This was as a special thank you for all the times he had taken care of Pepper when I had to go to an appointment. Cindy wasn't able to come though. She was having a bad time with her arthritis.

After launching the white boat, all three of us humans took turns steering it while our dogs mostly stayed put in it. We rode the waves for a spell. Then Robert turned off the motor and brought out fishing poles for everyone. Andy grabbed one and then handed another one to me.

"But it's been so long since I fished," I protested, as I took the fishing rod uneasily.

It was true that I hadn't dipped a line since the time I was a kid in Canada. Both of the men laughed at my apprehensions.

"I'll help you remember and do it right," said Andy.

Then my brother looked on with approval as my neighbor showed me how to bait the hook and then toss it in. As he did so, a passel of waterstriders scattered across on the river's still surface.

"Would you look at that!" said Robert as he pointed at the swift moving, long legged, water insects. "Those little guys are sure quick, aren't they?"

"Yes, they are and graceful too. That's why I like to make sketches of them," I agreed with amusement at the little scurrying creatures.

"Did you guys know that the Indians around here are the only ones who've made pictographs of those water skeeters? No one else has, anywhere," said Andy with a cheerful look on his broad, handsome face as he quickly threw his own line over the side of the boat. He had grown a long mustache and it was a good new look for him.

"I didn't know that, Andy. I'll have to look for some water-strider cave pictures next time I explore some caves," I said as I hurled my line in a few feet from where Andy had put in his.

"Let's all three of us go do some exploring for pictographs. Who knows, we might discover some new ones. Maybe even some depicting water skeeters," added my brother as he tossed in his line on the side of the boat opposite to where me and Andy were fishing.

"I can do that, I love going into caves. Takes me back to happy times in my childhood when me and my brother did that together," said Andy gleefully.

"I would like to do that too. You never know just what you'll find in the caves around here," I ventured with a playful laugh.

I was starting to feel better than I had since this whole cancer trip started. As it was, I hadn't laughed even faintly for over a month.

At that point, we humans stopped talking and waited to feel tugs on our lines. Meanwhile, our dogs walked about the boat, sniffing and exploring. At one point, Pepper found a piece of an old donut in a corner near the back of the boat. It was obviously a relic left over from a boat ride and picnic that Ozzy had taken me out on one summer.

Time passed and Andy felt a pull on his fishing line. Slick as a whistle, he began reeling it in and soon pulled up a good-sized trout that was flopping fiercely making big splashes on top of the water. He brought the fish unto the deck. It flopped for a few minutes and then was still.

"The first catch," I told him under my breath and he nodded.

But eight more were to follow. I even hooked one, amateur that I was. Time flew by and soon it was time to bring the boat in and roll it back on its hauler. Andy and Robert did this, while I loaded the dogs into my brother's SUV. I had all the fish in a large plastic bag. The three of us would divide them up equally among ourselves later.

After the boat had been docked and I was preparing to skip out of it with the dogs, I had looked down and saw a remarkable sight which I cannot explain to this day. There in the soft ripples was the image of a gray wolf. When I looked around me, however, he was nowhere to be seen and the image in the water had simply vanished.

DISASTER FOUR

I spent the next day leading up to my first chemo treatment under a dark cloud of apprehension, while outside the sky hung heavy with rain and clouds as black as the one shrouding my spirits. I went about my usual tasks, hiding my fears and worries and enduring the often misplaced sympathies of people who really knew just enough about their friends' and relatives' experiences with cancer to give me all the wrong advice and opinions.

"Go on the internet and find alternatives to chemo," advised one lady who was a fussy person with a grudge against all things medical.

Another woman, whose husband owned the local health store, was sure I was going to have a rough time of it. I learned in a hurry that it didn't pay to tell everyone about my condition. Some people were even callously indifferent to it. Like my old tormentor, Kandy Gasserbury.

I happened to be taking a break in between workouts at the gym on April 10th when I noticed her talking with Helen Brown Eagle, a white woman who shared my interest in the local Indian tribes. I gathered from their talk that Helen was having new problems with her heart. Wishing to tell her about my cancer and wanting to give her my support, I went over to join the conversation. I noticed how Mrs. Gasserbury glared at me before I even said a word. Still, I saw no reason why I shouldn't greet both of them. Bravely, I walked over to the two women and said "hello." Helen told me "hi" and was glad to see me, but Kandy just made a snarling sound and then bellowed, "What do you want, April!" I let that pass and starting talking with Helen. I told her about my cancer and she told me about what was going on with her, not just about her recent heart condition, but about some Indian ceremonies she had taken part in. The old vinegaroon left in a huff with her fists clenched. She didn't need to do that, there was plenty of room for all of us to talk together. But she didn't think I had the right to live, let alone be part of a conversation.

Once I was done talking with Hellen I went over to Mrs. Gasserbury and asked her why she was so rude to me. I knew why, but I thought it would do me some good to stand up for myself. I also tried to tell her about my cancer. But the woman had no compassion.

"You were very rude butting into my conversation with Helen like that!" she shouted while pointing her finger at me.

"Why are you so heartless? I could die of this cancer!" was my response. Perhaps it was a knee-jerk reaction on my part, but at that point I was feeling like I'd been pushed over the edge.

"Good riddance!" was her loud retort and I just walked out in a huff.

Perhaps she hadn't meant that last part, but I did. From that day on, I wouldn't speak to her or even look at her. I did my best to keep out of her way as I did my workouts which were to continue while my chemo treatments progressed. Mrs. Gasserbury, however, made some attempts to annoy me. She pushed a huge exercise bench in the way of the area where I did my benching. I just pushed it back. She turned the lights out in a room where I was doing planks. I turned them back on. She would make everything I wanted to sit on damp with cleaning solution. So I brought my own towel and wiped it dry each time. It was a constant dance. The stress of dealing with her was something I sure didn't need on top of my cancer diagnosis. The last straw came when the arrogant woman shouted an order at me.

"April, you must rack your weights instead of expecting other people to put them back for you!" she yelled at me after I was done benching.

I didn't answer back nor even look at her. I didn't comply with her demands that day either, but from then on I did try to be more diligent about putting the weights I'd used back where they belonged. But at that point, the blonde shrew had crossed a line. I complained about her to one of the ladies who owned the gym, explaining about my cancer condition and asking her to have a talk with Mrs. Gasserbury, to ask her to leave me alone. The woman, whose name was Chloe Baker, said that she would try to confront her about me, but that it might not happen anytime soon, because with their schedules, they hardly ever saw each other. Mrs. Baker also added that Mrs. Gasserbury was going away soon and that I might not ever see her again. That news did bring me some relief, although with my often dull, aching head, I neglected to ask her when my nemesis was going away and for just how long. When I insisted patiently that Mrs. Baker still talk with Mrs. Gasserbury, the lady became almost flippant.

"Try not to take anything she says too personally. Kandy is rough around the edges, but she's that way with everybody," said Mrs. Baker in a mild, but dismissive way.

The conversation left me feeling like I'd been let down. Still, I hoped that Mrs. Baker would eventually have a talk with the old vinigaroon about her treating me better, or at least not giving me a worse time than I was already having. I continued going to gym, though each morning before going there, I prayed for protection from the mean lady. Then finally, I stopped seeing her at all. I sincerely hoped that wherever she and her hangdog of a husband went, they would stay there forever.

Indeed, gymrat queens were the bane of my life. I will always believe that Valerie Kaine's cruel, closed-minded rejection of me from her gym started my cancer growing, while Kandy Gasserbury's persecution of me made it grow further.

Because of these and other hassles, my days and nights leading up April 30th were a hectic cycle of ups and downs. There were nights when I didn't sleep well at all. When the 30th finally rolled around, I felt like I was going to meet my own doom.

It was a damp windy day with rain threatening. I rode with my brother and sister-in-law to Shaxu, talking optimistically, but feeling a sense of dread. I checked in and was told to wait. As I waited, a man came and gave me a neck massage. He was one of the facility's comfort people, a part of the staff whose job it was to help cancer sufferers relax. I really appreciated his massage as my neck happened to be aching from some new exercises I had been doing and my muscles hadn't gotten used to yet. As the man, who was a fairly good-looking fellow in his fifties named Stan, gently took the tension from my neck, he talked with me about his farm which was just outside of The Dalles. I shared some of my own experiences growing up on a farm in the blue Canadian Rocky Mountain Range. In minutes, my tension was gone and I was feeling better. All this time, my brother had been watching the news on his smart phone, while Cindy played a computer game. When my massage was done, I thanked the fellow and started reading in a book I'd brought which was all about the Oregon Desert Region – its flora, fauna, and history.

The book, which was titled simply *The Oregon Desert* and was written by E. R. Jackman and R. A. Long, actually went into interesting detail about the area's ranches and the people who worked in them as cow hands and horse traders. I was just into an interesting account of an Indian fellow who made his living collecting wild horses and taming them when my name was called. Nurse Poule, who was a middle-aged type with graying hair, led me to a room and took my weight and other vital statistics. I was unhappy with my weight, but soon this nurse, who had already come across as a busy body from the phone call I had had with her, would make me feel worse. At the end of the exam, she turned to me with a suggestion I thought was highly out of place.

"So, you've decided not to have a port put in. I feel you're making a big mistake because it just makes it a lot easier for staff to take blood samples and administer intravenous medicines and its easier on you too. You won't be poked at all which many people find annoying," she told me in a way that she tried to make sound persuasive. I wasn't buying it.

"I don't want a port put in at this time," that was my decision and I was sticking to it.

With a resigned smile, the nurse directed me to the room where two technicians waited to take my blood samples. I said "hello" as I sat down and pulled up my arm sleeve. They had little trouble finding a vein in the hollow of my elbow pit. Even so, one of them did have the gall to say I needed a port as she worked on me. I pleasantly told her I was not going to have one put in at that time, even though I felt like smacking her hard. When the technicians decided they had taken enough of my blood, I was directed to another room where I was joined by my brother and sister-in-law. Together we met my new doctor, who was an Oncologist, that is a doctor whose medical expertise involved treating cancer and cancer alone. His name was Dr. Xiwang and to my delight and encouragement, he was an exceedingly good looking Asian. I had hit the jackpot there at Shaxu and felt that with him to guide me, my fighting this cancer was a sure victory. As an added bonus, Dr. Xiwang's manner was friendly and warm, as well as knowledgeable. He had a most beautiful and comforting smile.

Because I would be undressing to be examined from the neck down, my brother left the room, while my sister-in-law remained. The doctor looked over and felt the bumps on my breasts and armpits in a way that was gentle and professional. After the exam was done, I rebuttoned my blouse and my brother was invited back in. Dr. Xiwang then informed me that I was going to need a round of chemo treatments, six to be exact, since the cancer had spread. One of the places it had spread was to my liver where I had a cancerous spot less than an inch big. This caused me great alarm. I am a big David Bowie fan and was deeply grieved when he died of liver cancer. His album, *Blackstar,* which he made just before he died was loaded with songs themed about his own battle with this cancer. Blackstar is even the nick-name for cancerous lesions on the liver.

"Oh, no, not a blackstar! I have a blackstar then just like David Bowie!" I said in anguish as I covered my face with my hands and bent over with my elbows on my knees.

"It's true, doctor, he made that album full of songs that were just about his cancer," added my brother with a look of sympathy toward me.

"My sister-in-law doesn't have liver cancer, does she?" Cindy demanded to know. She wrapped her arms around me in a way that was protective as well as comforting.

Dr. Xiwang caught all of our moods and gave us a reassuring grin.

"No, it's nothing like that at all. David Bowie's condition was completely different from yours, April. You have breast cancer that spread to your liver. He had liver cancer that spread to his lungs and other parts of his body. Liver cancer is a lot more serious than breast cancer and the outcome is often not as good," he explained in comments that were meant for me but were directed to Robert and Cindy as well.

"Thank you, Doctor," I said with sincere relief.

It was then time for me to be hooked up to the intravenous device. I was also relieved that the good doctor hadn't made any comment about my needing to have a port put in. Obviously, he had better sense than the others and respected my individuality more.

The nurse led me to a very comfy padded easy chair, while Robert and Cindy took a couple of chairs near me. She explained that the whole thing would take four hours, but that I could get up and go to the bathroom if I needed to. This would be managed by having the intravenous bag attached to a patient transport trolley. I said "no thank you" to that wheeled device and was just content to hold off peeing until all my infusions were done. It wouldn't be hard for me to do that at all.

The first shot was a saline solution. This was followed by one of the biologics. Then the other biologic was administered. After the last biologic, they gave me a dose of an anti-nausea medicine, to counteract the stomach unsettling effects of the chemo, they told me. Finally, the chemo was put in my system.

All during this time, I read from my desert book, got a reiki treatment, and talked about the baldness is beautiful culture of Babylon 5's Centauri Race with a man named Clyde, who was a counselor from the center's comfort department. He was close to my age but was vigorous and quick moving, with gentle, understanding brown eyes and a nice mustache. Delightful company. I was not exactly having a happy time sitting there with the tube rammed in my arm, even so, I wasn't feeling that bad either. At the start, I felt a little dizzy and light-headed but it passed. The anti-nausea medicine must have done its trick because I did eat some fruit and drink some juice during the treatment. I expected to get violently ill and throw it all up, but I didn't. I didn't even feel queasy. The staff gave me a burp bag to use, but I never did.

At the end of the infusions, I had to pee really bad so I went to the nearest ladies room. I also brushed out my hair, which I was determined to enjoy caring for as long as I had it. I put on fresh lipstick wondering how much my cancer treatments were going to effect the way I looked. I heard that chemo made your skin dry. I would try not to be too concerned about that and just use more Oil of Olay, which I was applying liberally anyway along with a coat of Vaseline at bedtime. When I was done getting my face and hair prettied up, Robert took us for a meal at Tacos Del Rio. I didn't feel like eating much, but I was not talking to the toilet sick to my stomach either. I managed to down half an enchilada and small glass of pineapple Jarrito, a fruit-flavored soft-drink imported from Mexico. And I kept all this down the whole ride home and all through the night.

That night of my first cancer treatment, I was feeling tired, but not overly so. I even felt like taking Pepper for a walk all the way to the town's grain elevators, a half-mile jaunt. Even so, when I bedded down with her for the night, I thought of all the things that were missing from my life and started crying. Worse yet, in spite of the love from my dog and family, I began to wonder if all that cancer treatment was going to be worth it. I cried myself to sleep with Pepper nestled in my arms.

That night in my dream journey I was to meet someone very special. A new friend and guide who would teach me that my life was worthwhile and worth saving. His name was Billy Brave Salmon and he was from the Yakama People. My dream opened with me walking down the alleyway between the local Legion Hall and a number of stores. I came to an open area where a thrift store once stood and there was Billy sitting on a wooden packing crate with three puppets that were dressed in the beads, leathers, and feathers of his people. He was making them dance and sing on top of a packing crate draped with a rug woven with traditional Yakama designs.

"Áay! (Greetings!), April. I am Billy Brave Salmon and I have a special message just for you," he said as he gestured to a wooden crate near his make-shift stage which was draped with a gray, blue, and white blanket.

"You know my name," I said with deep wonder as I shook his hand and then settled down in the seat he indicated.

I admired his long black braids, short and stocky physique, and ornately beaded choker. From it dangled a gem carved in the shape of a salmon. He appeared to be in his late forties, though he could have been older, and his cinnamon complected face, though weathered from the elements and hardship, was still to me, exceedingly handsome. He smiled.

"I know much more about you, páysiks (friend). I know that you are very beautiful, both inside and out, but that you've always seen yourself as ugly. This is a wrong belief caused by the people you had around you as you were growing up. It is now time to cast aside all the wrong ideas you've believed since childhood," as he said this he demonstrated these truths by having a female puppet first hiding her face, acting out feelings of inferiority, and then casting away these notions.

This was symbolized by her tossing away a tiny woven basket full of dirt. I watched fascinated as well as enthralled.

65

"April, you will get better and you will find that this cancer trip has all been worth it, for you are destined to do worthwhile things," he continued now that he had that same lady doll punching down a monstrous puppet that represented my cancer.

It was hideous. A bent-over sickly-colored thing with long tentacle-like appendages like the kind cancerous growths use to attach themselves to parts of the body. The girl doll knocked the damned thing down to the ground, and it was "dead".

"Like what worthwhile things?" I wanted, no, needed to know.

"First you will win your battle with the cancer chílwitwapsúx (devil), while writing a little bit about it each day. Then you will turn this into a book which will be a best seller and will inspire others who are doing their own battle with cancer. From there, you who have always loved to make dolls, will set up a business where you sell them. Little girls will want these hand-sewn creations of yours. Grown women will want them too. You will make a lot of money while inspiring others to feel better about themselves," explained Billy as he worked the female doll to show her with a thread and needle sewing.

I was delighted and now had new respect for myself thanks to my new dream páysiks. But he had more. He had the doll put down her thread and needle and grab a tiny heart-shaped pillow and begin dancing with it. Throwing his voice, he had her singing a beautiful lilting melody, an Indian love song.

"April," said Billy as the puppet stopped singing, but kept dancing. "You will win all of your heart's desires when the Great Spirit over us all says the time is right."

"Even the love of a man and marriage," I asked hoping against hope.

"Especially the love of a man and marriage," said Billy.

Then the smoke of a dozen smudge sticks wafted up and he was gone. My dream ended on the happy throbs of Yakama tribal drums beating.

When I awoke the next morning, I felt happier and freer. Every problem I had was conquerable and I wanted to live and live life to the fullest. From then on, the sky was clear and blue, daffodils and tulips bloomed, and bird songs followed me wherever I went.

May 1st, the following day, was to be my happiest ever. I woke up early as usual, but though I felt a bit more tired than was typical, I still enjoyed my early morning jaunt with Pepper. We walked all the way to Ekone Park where there were wild lupines in the woods and every tree that was not a pine was in full leaf. We stood on some boulders that were high above The Little Klickitat River and admired how quickly it was flowing and how much its water level had risen since I had last seen it earlier in March.

"How high's the water, mama?"

"Five feet high and risin'," I sang out loud, quoting a Johnny Cash tune that Ozzy was very fond of.

The song, which was actually a musical account of a flood the singer had experienced as a boy, seemed to fit the situation, although The Little Klickitat was hardly at flood stage. After spending a few more minutes watching the river's waves crash over the stones and tree branches that lay in its bed, my dog and I began walking away from it. Soon we reached a slight grassy incline that led back onto the road.

After I got back with Pepper to our apartment, I had a quick breakfast and began working on a doll. Then I heard the phone ring.

"Hi, lil'sis, I know that it's the day after your chemo, but would you feel like going with me and Cindy to the local ice caves. Ask Andy if he would like to come along too. I'm bringing Henry and you two can bring your dogs," Invited my brother.

"Give me a moment to ask him. I'm sure he'd be interested," I said feeling very cheered by the suggestion.

Still holding my phone, I hurried downstairs to knock on Andy's door. When he opened his door and invited me in, I told him what Robert had in mind for the day.

"Yes, Skippy and I would like to see the ice caves," agreed my dear friend and neighbor, speaking into my cell phone. Robert gave him a friendly "hello".

When will you come and pick us up?" I asked after taking my phone back.

"At 11:00," replied my brother. It was only 9:30.

"Would that work for you, Andy?" I turned around and asked him.

"Yes," said my fellow tenant with a grin.

"We'll both see you at 11 then, beloved brother of mine," I said to him.

"I'll be there, so will Cindy and Henry," promised my brother.

When our call was done, I went and got Pepper and we spent an hour and a half visiting with Andy and his Chihuahua. I drank coffee with him while our two dogs played together and basked in the sunbeams that poured in from the window onto his balcony. He and I mostly talked about the times when each one of us paid visits to local ice caves. There was more than one such cave system in the Klickitat County area. When 11 came around, we received a call from my brother directing us to meet him in our apartment's back parking lot. We took our dogs down to his car where he and Cindy waited with a packed lunch. She had put beef sandwiches in her picnic basket along with corn chips and root beer. Andy and I both contributed to the meal. I brought some raw apricots, while he brought an apple pie he had baked.

We spent the whole day with our dogs touring an ice cave and we did see some intriguing pictographs in between the frigid glaze. There were no waterstriders etched on these particular stony walls. There were, however, a few depictions of wolves scrawled here and there. I took some pictures of them with my camera.

"A portent if ever there was one," remarked Andy. All of us agreed.

The whole trip through that frozen natural edifice in Trout Lake, Washington was a fun and rejuvenating experience for me, in spite of the heavy medicinal infusion I had taken the day before. I returned home feeling refreshed and inspired by it, so much so that I wrote an Edward Lear-style poem telling of the outing in detailed, but fanciful rhyme. It was titled, "Through The Ice Cave" and went as follows:

Through The Ice Cave
by April Berrigan

"Rare and fine,
Rare and fine,
Are the ice caves of Klickitat County;
Their floors are long and of ice do shine,
And of wonders they have quite a bounty;

69

I went to an ice cave on the 1st of May,
With my family, three dogs, and a friend;
We toured the cave the whole frigid way,
Eating apricots from the start to the end;

It was a bitter cold hike,
And our faces soon turned blue;
We found our way with a bright flashlight,
That helped us see ice bats fly through;

On the walls between the ice sheets,
Were pictures Native People had drawn;
Of hunters and animals running on swift feet,
And wolf spirits howling their wolf songs;

Ice icicles hung like stalactites from the ceiling stone cold,
While on the way out into the sun and light
We spied a huge toad with eyes wide and gold
He hopped and we followed him into a forest green and bright.

DISASTER FIVE

During the next few days after my first treatment, I did better than I expected too. Better than the people around me expected me too as well. I started to feel tired and beat up, but not so much that I couldn't do my regular chores and daily activities. I still took my dog for her walks, went to the store, and went to the mailbox. I even worked out at gym. I did my sewing and writing and stayed in touch with my loving family. Even so, I didn't visit much and found myself not doing things that I absolutely did not need or want to do.

As for nausea, it hardly troubled me at all. I had expected to be violently ill most of the time, but I only seemed bothered by severe stomach trouble at night and then only if I didn't respect my acid reflux. I did have stomach aches and didn't feel like eating a lot during the first week after treatment, but I still ate and kept my food down. That is, during the day. I might wake up with nocturnal vomiting spells. But that was nothing unusual for me. I'd been doing that for years before my chemo treatment. I tried taking the prescribed anti-nausea medication at night and it didn't seem to help my acid reflux at all. So I quit taking it. I seemed to do well enough without it anyway. Besides the stomach settling remedy made me severely constipated, like I had stone blocks in my upper intestinal tract. This was painful and more trouble than it was worth. On the sly, I used enemas to clean myself out and threw out the remedy. It was back to antacids and soda mixed with water, though I didn't need to use these every night either.

The sores that were supposed to erupt in my mouth never did. I did feel some soreness and abrasion near my gums during the first week after treatment, but it quickly left. The ½ teaspoon baking soda in ½ cup of water that I took as an occasional stomach remedy probably helped keep the mouth sores from developing.

I was often tired and took a lot of naps, but other than that, life went on fairly normal for me. Other people were amazed that I was doing so well. Some were skeptical to the point of being negative. Joseph Holmes, owner of the local health food store was one of the latter.

"You better look out, April," he cautioned. "You're feeling okay because you just started, but further down the line, that chemo is liable to knock you for a loop."

"I'll just deal with it if it does. But I would appreciate it if you could be more positive. I need all of the positive support I can come by right now," was my defensive retort.

"I know a lady who went through chemo and didn't feel bad at all," said tall gangly Mr. Holmes who suddenly realized he needed to change his tune with me. "Her hair all fell out, but she felt fine through the whole treatment.

I smiled knowing that the man meant well, he was just the product of a religious background that sometimes frowns on medical doctors. His remark reminded me that my hair hadn't started to fall out yet. I dreaded the day that it did, but knew I could handle that too. I had already ordered a beautiful, natural-looking wig from a woman at Shaxu whose job was to supply women with wigs who had lost their hair to chemo treatments. I would receive that blonde hair piece at the time I would need it the most, when my hair started thinning af-ter the second treatment. I also got a bunch of wigs from an

72

acquaintance named Chris who had had a double mastectomy and now worked as a counselor for women battling cancer. Some people had promised me wigs, but hadn't delivered. It didn't matter, I was secure that I would have more than enough hair pieces. Besides, the doctor assured me that my hair would grow back when the chemo stopped.

My greatest strength and hope came from my dream friend, Billy Brave Salmon. He would use his puppets to demonstrate that my life was worth living and that there were better things down the road of life for me. He also used his puppets to teach me valuable traditional skills. In my nocturnal meetings with him, he would often bring out a female puppet he named Máts'ya (Calico Salmon)who would cut loose her strings and then show me how to weave baskets of all sizes. In the days that followed, my creations showed truly fine workmanship and Billy was very pleased. Making these dream baskets soon became a true pleasure. There were other, unexpected positive results as well. With Billy's medicine working through Máts'ya I soon found that weaving baskets was weaving my entire life together. Gradually, I found myself becoming better coordinated, physically, mentally, and emotionally. I was developing normal reflexes. I also became capable of reading facial expressions and non-verbal cues from other people, something I was never able to do since early childhood.

To my added joy, I found myself weaving baskets that soon showed the fine skills of the baskets I wove in my dreams. I made them with my own designs and started selling them at the local Saturday Market which was starting to go into full swing now that it was springtime. Along with my dolls, clothes, and books, beautiful woven baskets made of local materials became a prime selling item for me. And it wasn't just because of the fine work that went into them, it was also because my interpersonal skills were developing, being woven together to finally make me whole.

Indeed, every meeting with Billy and his puppets was a pleasure and increased my feelings of strength and well-being which radiated all through my daily life. Because of him, the sun was shining bright and the waves of the nearby Little Klickitat River gleamed with golden sparkles whenever me and my dog walked past it. Soon, there would be a patch of purple lilies blooming in a grassy spot along the trail there. Orchestras of crickets serenaded us as we strolled through the deepest part of the woods near the gushing body of water.

The sweetness of May was in the air. Then came my next chemo treatment on the 21st of that fair month. Every prospect looked good, my tumors were already shrinking.

When I was taken to the lab at Shaxu where they took the blood samples, one of the technicians insisted on taking them from a spot in the middle of my arm, not from a vein in the hollow of my elbow or from my wrists. On the first try, on my left arm, her needle encountered a vein that didn't work.

"She blew, she blew!" exclaimed the technician out loud as my blood spurted ineffectually.

Then she starting poking into my right arm with better results. She also used a blood pressure cuff to make my veins stand out better.

"This spot is the only one used for taking blood samples and hooking you up intravenously," said the technician a she pointed to the needle in the middle of my left arm while extracting the blood. "I'll just leave the tube in you when I'm done.

When she and the other woman had taken the blood samples I was led by another nurse to a room where she put me through the whole rigamarole of taking my temperature, blood pressure, and so forth. My brother and sister-in-law were there to give me comfort. When the nurse was done, I sat and talked with them. Soon, we were joined by the capable, charming Dr. Xiwang.

"The tumors in my breasts and armpits have really shrunk down. I feel so much better and most of the pain is gone," I explained with a hopeful grin.

"Good, let's have a look," he said returning my grin with one as sweet as honey. Then he had me take off my blouse and lay down. Of course, my brother left the room to wait in the lounge at that point.

"They have gone way down," said Dr. Xiwang, who seemed a little amazed at my progress. "and your left breast isn't full of red lumpy spots anymore. You are responding very well to treatment."

"Thank you for your help," I said delighted that I seemed to be already on the mend.

"It's good to know that she's already on the road to surviving this cancer," added Cindy.

"I see real progress in her case. All she needs to do is keep on with her treatments and her getting better is a sure thing," reassured Dr. Xiwang as he finished the exam and then had me put my blouse and bra back on.

With Cindy beside me, my oncologist had a nurse lead me back to the infusion room where my brother had been waiting for me. I took a seat near one of the infusion machines. During this interim, the massage man came and gave me a good neck and back rub. As he gently took the tension out of me, he explained about his strawberry plants and how they were growing.

"Up in the hills in Canada, my folks and I had some really good strawberry plants. There were also some growing wild," I said, feeling momentarily blissful over the berry-sweet memories.

The fellow and I talked a little bit more about strawberries and the different varieties of them. All too soon, a nurse came over to hook me up to my initial medicine bag and the massage and strawberry memories came to a stop.

"You really should get a port. It would make it a lot easier for me to do this,' said the nurse in a mildly scolding way as she connected me to the infusion device.

"I will not have a port installed at this time. Maybe someday further down the road," I answered patiently, but still feeling a bit cornered.

My veins took the medicine well that day of my second chemo and biologic treatment. The first time was four hours, this was three, but it was still tedious. I read in my book about Oregon deserts and talked with my brother and Cindy. Soon, it was noon and the lady in charge of handing out lunches and snacks came by. But I declined, there was something special I wanted my family to do for me. I wanted them to go to the local Safeway and pick up some egg foo young soup. The store sold it in a deli section along with a good selection of other Chinese food items. I also wanted potato salad. I gave them the money for this food and told them to get some for themselves as well. They asked me if I would be okay if they left me. I assured them that I would be, so they took my money and went to Safeway. In a short while, they returned with the oriental soup and potato salad and ate it with me. Thank God, I wasn't nauseous. A special stomach-settling medicine that came with my infusions helped with that. Later, it would make hell to pay with constipation, but in the meantime, all was well on my digestive front. I had requested these particular food items on the advice of a nephew whose own daughter had done a round of chemo.

"That soup and potato salad made her stomach really settle down," he had explained.

But although the effect of eating this food wasn't quite so dramatic, I did enjoy the meal as I sat there enduring the infusion. After the meal, I returned to my book, while Robert and Cindy entertained themselves with their smart phones – him with messages and her with a card game.

When the course of my treatment was complete, I was unhooked and left with my brother and sister-in-law. I was feeling a bit tired and sore, but overall not too poorly. I was even able to go shopping at Grocery Outlet, Joann Fabrics, and Fred Meyers.

Back home, though, I noticed some features that disturbed me. One was a big, black, blue, and purple bruise on my right arm where the lab technicians had made a botched attempt to hook me up. On the other arm, where they had actually succeeded in putting in the infusion tube there was a two-inch long burn. I hadn't recognized it as such in the beginning and it didn't hurt. I started putting cold pads alternately on both wounds and they felt well. At this time, I thought of how the technicians had initially put the infusion tube in the hollow of my elbow pit. I also thought of the marks left on my arms. All of these unpleasant developments made me wonder if the technicians might not all be trying to maneuver me into taking a port. Disturbed by that thought, I phoned Katie and aired my fears that the technicians might just be giving me a bad time because I was holding to my wish not to have a port installed.

She told me that was unlikely. That the women were going by the book, so to speak, but weren't trying to pressure me into anything. She also added that some of them might be dolts, but meant well. If they bruised me, they didn't have ulterior motives for doing so. She reminded me that a few of them go strictly by what they learned in medical school, but that I needed to stand my ground with them.

"If you've made up your mind you don't want a port, tell them so. If they only go by what they learned in medical college, how can they learn anything if you don't tell them how you feel? And remember you're their patient. That means it's their job to help you and go along with what you want," she added with strong emphasis.

"Good point, Katie. And what's more, my not having a port put in has led to added health benefits," I explained.

"Oh, tell me, auntie."

"It mostly has to do with my water intake. Because drinking more pure water helps my veins plump up, I really work at getting six to eight glasses in every day. If I did take a port, I would just go back to my bad habits of only drinking one or two glasses of water a day. That's because with a port installed, I would feel what's the need? No matter how dehydrated I get, the port will still work. But because I want to avoid needing a port at all costs, I will keep my water intake up."

"Good for you. I drink eight glasses a day myself and have for a long time. Be sure to tell the technicians what you just told me and I think they'll understand you better."

"Pray for me that I will be able to think clearly enough and explain myself clearly enough at my next appointment so I will be able to get my point about the water across."

"Oh, I think you will, auntie. I have faith in you and you're strong. Try to have some faith in yourself."

"Thank you, Katie. You've made me feel a whole lot better and more determined."

After that talk, I did truly feel stronger and better able to stand my ground.   In the days to come, the bruise and the burn both healed.

DISASTER SIX

In the days following my second chemo and biologics treatment, I did fairly well with the every day routine of my life, all things considered. On the third day afterward I did have a vomiting spell at night and I did have some stomach aches during the days afterward, but I was able to keep my food down following that one acid reflux episode. I just didn't feel like eating and drinking a lot, so I didn't. I did manage to get all of my vitamins and my water quota down and keep it down. Ondansetron, the anti-nausea medication that they gave me during the infusion made me as constipated as all get out, but that passed, in more than one manner of speaking. I did have intestinal cramps during the constipation spell, but a hot pad helped with that. Also, taking warm water in my bowels and holding it for ten minutes. At one point, I asked a man friend what to do about lagging bowels and he suggested lots of apple juice and plenty of ripe cherries (a lot nicer alternative to prunes and prune juice). I was on the verge of trying both, when my bowels corrected themselves. Thankfully, I also never got the headaches that Ondansetron was supposed to cause. I was also taking a mild steroid to prevent the chemo from causing my feet and hands to swell. It was supposed to make me feel wired and unable to slept well, but it didn't. I only took this medicine on the day before, the day of, and the day after, chemo treatment and I was sleeping like a log.

When it came to energy, I was about normal, although I did find myself needing to take a lot of naps, especially during the week following the treatment. At this time, however, there was a look-down thing that happened. My hair started thinning and then it fell out in clumps. I used some of it to make a summer time doll in a yellow dress. I drew green leaves all over the cotton fabric before I cut out and sewed the doll's dress. I also made little sandals for it that I sewed green beads on. The face was embroidered and I made a head band of green leaf-shaped sequins to hold its hair in place. This coif was a bit harder to manage than the kind of materials that I've been used to making doll hair out of, mainly yarn and embroidery floss. But I was able to glue my hair on and have it look fairly neat. The girls at my local beauty parlor were impressed by the doll when I showed it to them during an appointment to have all the stubble shaved from my head and my eyebrows dyed and plucked. Thank God, I still had my eyelashes and eyebrows.

At that point, I started to wear the wig I got from Shaxu whenever I went anywhere, like to the post office or the grocery store. Around the house and at gym, however, I would wear one of my turbans with a pair of dangly earrings. People told me that I still looked lovely. I had rough time believing them, but their words did give me comfort and assurance.

I kept on with my job with Mr. Peterson and did well at it.

"Your working for me is a big favor to me, not the other way around. If it wasn't for your housework, I'd just be batching it and my place would really show it," he told me after I was done with my latest round of work.

I smiled and thanked him. Since I had started working for him, I had only been doing it once every two weeks. It was just as well. Now that schedule was about all I could afford, energy wise. My job at the art gallery I had to give up for the duration. Two jobs while enduring this cancer treatment was more than I could handle.

Still, my spirits were up and I wasn't lagging emotionally. Billy and his puppet shows and words of wisdom helped with that.

In one dream late in May, Billy did a show with a puppet I recognized well. It looked exactly like a Yakama doll I had made for the grand daughter of a man who lived downstairs and who I sometimes also did chores for. Billy had this doll dance and sing for me. I was elated that he was using a puppet so like one of my handmade creations. After the show I felt very proud of myself and my abilities. Then he put the puppet away and gave me even more encouragement.

"April, you have evolved and are on your way to achieving your apex as a person. But never forget that you, your writing, and your art will always be evolving," as he told me this, Billy gave me a necklace made of clay and wooden beads with a gemstone salmon attached in the middle. Then my dream ended.

Three days later, I found a necklace just like it laying beside of a road. I picked it up and started wearing it and found that when I wore it, it brought me a special charm. Men and women of all ages started to complement me on my appearance. Something that never happened to me ever, not even when I was younger. Especially not when I was younger. My book sales started picking up, but not in great sums of money.

"That will only happen with your cancer book," Billy assured me in a dream just before my third appointment at Shaxu. It would fall on June 11. Following that one, I would be half-way through my tiresome treatment program.

I found the June 11 appointment even more onerous than the one previous since I had to go to it extra early. Because it was slated for 8:45 am this necessitated me waking up and getting Pepper taken care of earlier than usual. Then I had to get myself ready for the trip, which was never a simple, easy task. I have never traveled well and preparing for a trip of any length has always taken a lot out of me. Then too, whenever I packed for a journey, if I was to take five items along, I would inevitably bring four and leave at least one behind. This still happened even when I made up lists and planned ahead. To compound it all, I have never been well-organized in the morning and the effects of the medicine infusions were making me even less so.

Even so, I managed to miserably get myself together and be picked up at 7:30 am. When I got my ride with Robert and Cindy, I swore that I would make other arrangements in the future. My brother had insisted that we take the 8:45 am appointment and I hadn't protested because it had been just after my chemo treatment and I was still dazed by it. But as we rode to the appointment, I shook off my early-morning tiredness and made a request.

"Robert, I'll go this early this time, but from now on could we go less early?" I asked with a fretful yawn.

"Yes, lil'sis, but we have to go early this time, because I have an appointment of my own to go to here in The Dalles. I have to see my dentist at 9:30. I couldn't get an earlier appointment and I have a couple of molars and one front tooth with cavities big enough to put my fist through," my brother explained as he opened his mouth and pointed at his bad teeth.

I looked closely. They were indeed in awful shape.

"That's fine, beloved brother of mine. Sometimes we all have to combine schedules. And you really need to have those teeth taken care of. I bet they hurt," I said, trying to sound sympathetic in spite of my own distress.

"Only when I laugh," said Robert with a touch of painful humor.

"I probably won't be able to go this early every time. It's rough on me to get up with the crack of dawn and have to roust around. This chemo stuff has made me the opposite of an energetic lark," I continued feeling like I had been dragged through a knot hole.

"You won't need to. This will probably never happen again during the rest of your treatment," said my brother kindly.

"No, don't worry about it," chimed in Cindy.

Even though my brother and sister-in-law's words were a comfort, I was still feeling out of sorts.

When I got to Shaxu, I was in a bad mood, though I was trying to temper it. I was determined to tell the lad technicians that I'd made up my mind once and for all not to have a port put in, so could they please not mention it. I also planned on telling them about how my not wanting to have a port installed encouraged me to drink at least six glasses of water each day.

Cindy waited for me in the lobby, as my brother left me for the dentist.

"I will be back to check on you when the tooth yanker is done with me," he assured me with a bit of sardonic jesting.

"I'll be here the whole while, April," said my sister-in-law.

I smiled. Then I got a temporary frown as I thought of my appointment at the lab. I hoped that they wouldn't give me a bad time about anything that day. I was even less in the mood for it than usual.

Determined and with my nicest fake grin, I checked in with the receptionist. Then I joined my sister-in-law in waiting in the lobby. I read some more in my desert book, while she played a card game on her smart phone. On the plus side, both of us got massages that day, something that made me feel vastly better.

When it was time, I was led into the room where my blood samples would be taken. Before I let them take a drop, I explained my feelings – about how not having a port installed was encouraging me to adopt better health habits. In particular drinking healthy amounts of water. After I was done, the two women looked at each other like they found my attitude a bit puzzling. I suppose they were thinking, she should drink at least six to eight glasses of water anyway. But they kept that opinion to themselves and went along with my wishes to not mention my need for a port again.

I followed that up by stressing that in the beginning one of them had chosen the hollow under my elbow for the infusion.

"Is there any reason why, at this point, I have to take my infusion in the center of my arm instead of say, under my elbow?" I asked, trying to sound firm, but mild.

They then went on to explain that it just made it easier for them to put it in the center of my arm. They also gave me the usual talk about how it would be a lot less harsh on my veins which could be irritated. I noted that they said nothing this time about my veins possibly being burned and corroded, just irritated. I was already feeling irritated so being physically irritated would seem like a small nuisance at this point. Besides, I would be half-way through my treatment at this point, so I felt that if serious corrosion was going to happen, it would have already happened by now. So I stood my ground on wanting to take the infusion from my elbow hollow. They complied with me, but one of them did express a complaint.

"Seriously, April, your veins are a challenge," the technician said in mild protest as she daubed my elbow hollow with sterilizing solution and then slipped in the needle-bearing tube. It went in with great ease to her and my relief. I hoped that that proved I'd won my point.

From there, I was led to a room where my vitals were taken *again*. Then I was told to wait, my Doctor Xiwang would be in shortly. I was joined by my sister-in-law and she read a magazine while I read in my desert book. A half an hour later, Dr. Xiwang came in looking all elated. With him was an intern. To my vast pleasure, she was an Asian too.

"Meet my assistant Lucy Phong," said Dr. Xiwang as he introduced her to Cindy and me. "She's here to take notes because your response to treatment has not been just good, it's been phenomenal."

We both shook hands with Ms. Phong and then he told me to disrobe from the top down.

"All my tumors feel like they're completely gone," I said as I unbottoned and then laid aside my pink blouse along with my bra.

"Very good. Let's check you out," said my doctor as he and his assistant examined my breasts and armpits while Cindy looked on with care and interest. Sure enough, the tumors had shrunk down and then disappeared.

"Can medicine alone do that?" I asked, feeling a bit better than I had before.

"Yes, and from the way you are responding so well to it, after these last two treatments, you will be going on some hormone blockers and antibodies and that will be all you will need to do

86

from then on," Doctor Xiwang told me as his assistant grinned sweetly. Cindy and I were also grinning. This was great good news.

After this meeting, Cindy and I were led to the infusion room. In minutes, Nurse Poule came and hooked me up. I wasn't given any barf about needing a port, but I was made to have my infusion arm bandaged to a board.

"Is this really necessary?" I asked.

"It's needed so you don't bend your elbow and cause the infusion to go wrong," she replied.

I sighed, fighting back suspicions that she was doing this board trip to punish me for insisting on not having a port and having the infusion tube placed in my elbow socket. During the hours I sat there, trying to read my book, my brother came back. This time he was the one who looked like the biblical camel that had been dragged through the eye of a needle. Obviously, his ordeal with the dentist had been a rough one. He still managed a smile as he squeezed my hand and then took a chair beside of Cindy.

Two other people also made my ordeal a little brighter. They were Marge Ogden and her son Carl. Mrs. Ogden was a weight lifter who had also been working out at The Steel Horse Gym and I had had a following out with her. This was largely the fault of Mrs. Kaine, however. The gym instructor had insisted that Marge contact me by facebook and "straighten me out" according to how she saw a certain matter. In response, I had blown up defensively at Marge, who had been a good friend to me up until that time. I didn't appreciate the tall, robust, blonde lady accusing me, under Mrs. Kaine's directions, of being frustrated about not having a ride to a weight lifting competition that was coming up in Portland because I wanted to compete. It just wasn't true. I didn't want to compete. I just wanted to attend the event while sitting in the audience. Because, Marge had gone along with everything that Kaine said against me, we became bitter enemies. We unfriended each other and wouldn't communicate in any way, shape, or manner. She accused me of being "delusional", while I accused her of being an "old meanie".

But then she got breast cancer. She then stopped working out at the gym and I forgave her. At first I was tentative about reconciling with her and went about it in slow and easy steps. I saw her outside her house, looking very peeked and with her lovely hair gone and I would say "hello". She would say "hello" back. Then we would carry on conversations. These usually weren't very long to start with though. This wasn't because she still hated me, but because she was feeling ill from her chemo treatment. I would bring her cards and she would smile at me through her pain. There were days when I would visit her and play with her cats. She had a large bevy of them. Then she was letting me in her place for a snack. I would ask how she was doing and she would always try to sound upbeat.

"I have my good days and my bad days. But I'm facing this cancer and fighting it like a girl," she would insist.

Indeed, she would make the words and title of the song "Fight Like A Girl" by Anti Cochran her own motto and words of faith to heal by. When it came my time to fight the same battle, I would gain similar inspiration from the same song. As it was, Marge had a banner made with the words, "fight like a girl" printed across it and put this banner on her little yellow jeep. She also had pink T-shirts made that proclaimed that same fiery message.

Marge had had a job as a postal worker delivering mail for years before her cancer. Unfortunately, she was now forced to take a break from her job as she recovered. Even so, every time I saw her, she looked stronger and more able. I once caught her and her son doing some yard work with their rose bushes which bloomed in perfusion on their property. She looked like she was getting her color back along with her hair.

Her son was a thoughtful man of about thirty who was a computer genius. I often hired him to help me when I encountered a computer-related problem or task that was beyond my abilities. During the summer before my own cancer diagnosis, I had met them both at the local Community Days Parade. It was good to see her out and about, waving at the floats and talking with people. In between the events, I had a good visit with her and Carl. I had to smile when on one occasion, Marge, who really has nice legs showed them off to some guys that she knew who were riding a float. It was good to see her getting back her self-confidence regarding her looks. She had more than I had and my hair was still intact at that time.

Then I got the crud and my visits and most of my outings stopped. As was typical, I didn't feel like visiting anybody or going to parades while I was going through my own chemo treatments. I still prayed for Marge though.

And she was not to be gone from my life either. On the day of my third chemo treatment, as I sat enduring the medicine flow through its tube into my system, who should I see walk in but Marge and Carl. To my delight, her blonde hair had grown back, although she had dyed it blue which I thought was a rather sweet touch. Both of them said "hello" to me and gave me hugs. I introduced them to my brother and sister-in-law.

"I bet you never expected to see me in here, of all places," I told the mother and son with a bit of pain-edged humor.

"Don't worry about it, April, stick with the program and you'll be fine," Marge reassured me with a kind smile.

"But I'm stage four with my breast cancer," I revealed with a little fear.

"That doesn't matter nowadays. I believe you'll be fine. Heck, there were days that I thought I wasn't going to make it, but look at me now," said Marge with an exuberance born of better health.

I smiled. Her remark really did make me feel a heap better.

She got to talking with one of the nurses there, evidently someone whom she had been working closely with during her own cancer struggle. Carl sat down and started talking with me. He is tall and blond just like she is and has her interest in lifting weights and collecting cats. He is also a huge science fiction fan and we chatted awhile about Babylon 5's Centuri Race and their bald is beautiful traditions. A long time watcher of the program, Carl had learned a few facts that I was unaware of.

"The men of that alien race are bald too. They just wear hair pieces," he revealed. We both chuckled about that.

Then we got talking about 3-D computer printers, since computers happen to be his third passion in life, after working out and cats. At that point, he placed a special knick-knack in my hands, one that he had made on his own 3-D printer.

"I made this for you, April," he said coyly.

I looked at the item, which was made of light golden-yellow plastic. It was in the shape of an octopus. This was very significant because years ago, while still living in Midway, British Columbia, Canada, I had received the message from the spiritual realm that I would someday come by a small item in the shape of an octopus. What's more, I would receive it at the time when I needed it the most. Something similar had happened years before. I was told that I would find the image of a black horse in some unexpected way. Sure enough, months later, I found a plastic horse which happened to be four inches long and solid black in the ditch along the side of a local church. Now I had my octopus!

I thanked my friend who clasped my hand and told me to be brave.

"You are on the road to healing from this. You can win, I know you are already," he said. Just at that moment, his mother told him they needed to hurry back to Goldendale.

"The cats need to be fed," she reminded him. Then they each gave me a last hug along with some encouraging words and were out the door.

My brother and Cindy then spent the rest of the infusion session talking about my friends and admiring the toy octopus Carl had made for me.

When the whole ordeal was done, I was told to come back to Shaxu on July 2nd. Thankfully this time I would be coming for my infusions at 10 am. Before taking me home, Robert treated me and Cindy to a meal at Denny's. I had a fish sandwich and a glass of milk.

Later on that night, I threw up. But that was nothing new to me and had its *ooky* origin more in emotions than in an actual stomach upset. I took some soda in water and my belly settled back down. Drinking that was good insurance against mouth sores anyway.

That night, with my stomach all calmed down, I had a dream that was absorbing and carried a serious message. In it, I was watching with delight and amusement as Billy had two of his puppets, which were done in the forms of two Yakama boys, both supposedly younger than 10, doing a gambling game. They were using an assortment of sticks, smooth pebbles, and the skulls of small birds. I even noticed they were using round marbles made of local tan-colored clay. What a hoot! When their game was done, Billy laid his boy puppets aside and turned to me with a serious look on his handsome sorrel face.

"April, you can gamble with sticks, stones, bones, and marbles, but you must never again gamble with your health. When you didn't go and have mammograms done starting at age forty, you were gambling with your health," he said pointedly.

I promised him guiltily that I would never gamble with my health again.

Then as June neared July, Marge would reach me in another way that I found touching and encouraging. The week following my latest chemo treatment, I was walking into the Post Office and was given a special card from her along with a couple pairs of lovely earrings. On the cover of the card was a message about sending me hugs, while the picture on it showed Charlie Brown hugging his dog, Peanuts. She signed it all over with positive messages about "God loving me" and that she was "thinking of me". I was touched and inspired by Marge's kindness, so I made her a thank you card with a picture I drew of her favorite cartoon character, Tweety Bird. In fact, she is so fond of this feisty little yellow canary that she named her yellow vehicle after him and has his picture on the jeep's back window.

DISASTER SEVEN

June rolled over into July and then it was time for my fourth
appointment at Shaxu. I had decided to go with my acquaintance, Chris, this time since she had asked to take me and I
thought I should give my brother and sister-in-law a break.
The thin lady with the short brown hair done in a pixie hair-
do came and got me in her white SUV. She had her teenage
daughter, Debbie with her. It all started out pleasantly enough.
Debbie was sweet rather than offish to me. She even went and
got me a bottle of water to drink on my journey. I had been apprehensive about meeting Debbie and riding with her. Because
she happened to be seventeen, I feared she might be rude and
offish. But Debbie apparently had been raised not to be that
way with someone just because they happened to be chronologically older. Indeed, some parents think it's cute when their
teenagers are mean and rude to someone older than them.

"Oh, they're just asserting themselves," these parents say.
"It's all a normal part of their growing up. They have to defy
authority and anyone older than them represents authority to
them."

I have always felt that such parents need to be horsewhipped.
I didn't choose to be the age that I happened to be trapped
in, indeed, I have felt my age since turning forty to be a dire
embarrassment. So if someone younger is going to pick on
me for being older, thus relegating me to the position of being
an authority figure I have no desire to be in in the first place,

I am left with the feeling of being trapped in a war between the generations I have no stomach for fighting. I have always liked to get along with everyone on an equal basis, regardless of chronological age. Hell, when I was in my teens, I even gravitated to persons much older then myself, persons in their forties and fifties. I thought they had the most interesting stories to tell, especially elders, men and women, who had spent years in the Yukon. As a kid growing up in the mountains of Canada, I would sit for hours as they spun out accounts of their adventures as trappers and gold panners. Certainly, I had dear friends my own age too and younger. I will always remember with fond feelings the times I hiked and played games along the local creeks with a couple of Indian girls, both of whom happened to be my age peers. With such inter-generational openness in my background, it isn't surprising that I am highly turned off by the typical attitude of persons, both young and older that poisons relations between different age groups in the twenty-first century. Happily, Debbie was an exception. She and I talked about our dogs and we got along fine. I found out that she had four.

At one point, Debbie starting talking with her mother about problems she was having at work. She had a job at the city's Subway sandwich place. I thought Chris handled talking with her very well. She gave her advice about believing in herself and over looking the flaws of others. I said nothing, but listened with interest.

When we had driven into The Dalles, Chris dropped her daughter off at Subway. Then she drove on to Shaxu. Chris stood with me as I checked in and I found out that she had a lot of friends at the cancer center. This made sense as she had once worked at MCMC which was in the same neighborhood. She sat with me as we waited for me to be called into the lab. As we waited, the massage man came and gave me a good rub down on my neck and back. That was very good since I had woken up with bad aches in my neck, shoulders, and upper back. He also told me in a soft voice all about how his raspberry harvest was doing. He had been selling raspberries by the bushel. His garden talk and the massage did the trick. When he was done, I was feeling a lot better. He asked Chris if she wanted a massage as well, but she refused with a coy grin.

Just then the nurse called me to come in and have my blood work done, thank God no talk of ports this time. There was, however, a slight dispute. One of the technicians, who happened to be a new girl, attempted to put the infusion in the middle of my arm. When I suggested the elbow region, the other technician, who had been working with me all along, told her that they had been using the elbow hollow. She did have to put in her technical two-cents though.

"We don't like putting it in the elbow area, because there's always a chance the medicine could go into the joint. We have to keep careful track to make sure it doesn't happen," she said as the other technician inserted the needle-bearing tube.

"Very good, but I'll take my chances," I replied sweetly, but insistently.

When my infusion tube was in place, my heart beat, blood pressure, and so forth were taken by a nurse. I then waited to talk with the glowing, brilliant, Dr. Xiwang. Since I was finished with my book about the desert in Oregon, I read from *The Centerville Ghost,* a chilling mystery set in the small but history-rich community of Centerville, Washington. Finally, I was joined by my doctor, who examined me and told me that my response to the medicine I was getting was exceptional.

"At the rate you're going, you'll just need to do the last two treatments and then we'll put you on a hormone blocker," he said with a smile of genuine enthusiasm.

"What are hormone blockers and why are they necessary?" I asked, my curiosity peaked.

"Hormone blockers are crucial to preventing your cancer from coming back. In your case, the tumors were receptive to estrogen, progesterone, and HER2 and blocking these hormones prevents them from attaching themselves to the areas where your tumors were and starting them up again," explained my doctor with patient precision.

"Okay," I said, then shifted the topic. "Could medication alone rid me of cancer, advanced as it was?"

"Yes, but it's unusual for that to happen. What has happened in your case is a miracle," he told me in a voice full of enthusiasm.

"Yes, I believe in miracles. But I also believe that I am healing so well because of your medical genius. Thank you for your good doctoring and wonderful smiles. You have a beautiful smile that lights up the world."

"Thank you, April. I will keep doing everything in my corner of the world to rid it of cancer. That will keep me smiling."

"You have already done that with me and I'll always be grateful to you."

At the end of our meeting, I wanted to kiss the good doctor who was really quite a handsome man as well as a physician of great medical expertise. But I contented myself with only shaking his hand in gratitude. Towards the tail end of our conversation, Dr. Xiwang mentioned something about me needing to go on a form of medicine called antibodies along with the hormone blockers. Unfortunately, my foggy brain hadn't picked that last part up. It often let me down like that.

After I left Dr. Xiwang, I was joined by Chris. Together, we were led by a nurse to a special room set apart from the infusion room. I agreed to sit there and be hooked up. Halfway through my treatment, I was to regret that decision. The room was chillingly cold and I had come in pink shorts and a pink tank top. Even so, I wouldn't notice just how cold the room was until hours later. The nurse gave me a preheated blanket and began the hooking up process. She was new and Nurse Poule was with her, acting as an overseer. Together they got me attached to the machine and then left me. I was very annoyed that they had my infusion arm bandaged down to a board since it made all movement difficult, including turning the pages of my book. I asked them why that had to encumber me that way.

"We don't want you bending your arm even a little because it could cause your infusion tube to come undone. I would hate for that to happen," replied Nurse Poule.

"You mean you don't have a port?" asked Chris.

In response, I rolled my eyes and sighed. I was tempted to ask her if she had a port, but figured I already knew what her answer would be. *Of course.*

Chris and I chatted about the book I was trying to read, then she excused herself. She had some errands to run. I told her, "See ya later" and returned to trying to read my book. It was difficult, not just because of the pinning down of my right arm, but also because they had given me a different anti-nausea medication. As part of the infusion, they had given me Prochlorperazine instead of Ondansetron as a stomach-settler. I had insisted on the medicine switch-over because Ondansetron had made me so severely constipated. I would regret this in the days to come. Prochlorperazine, which is also a powerful anti-psychotic, would make me feel more drained than usual.

In the meantime, I did a lot of naps right there in my infusion chair. I also tried to apply myself to my book, but due to the drowsiness caused by the Prochlorperazine could barely catch what I was reading. I also tried talking with Chris, but found keeping track of a conversation difficult.

Hours later, my ordeal was over. They removed the board, pulled out the tube, and let me leave my chair to go to the receptionist's desk where I was informed that my next appointment would be on the 2 of that same month at ten o'clock. Though feeling so tired that I could barely drag myself around at that point, I was still elated that my next appointment would not be as early as the second one had been.

As I started on the trip back to Goldendale, all I wanted to do was sleep. Debbie seemed to understand that better than her mother who persisted in carrying on a conversation. But at least she was someone who seemed to understand me and where I was coming from. For instance, when I explained to her that a HUD inspection was coming up and I felt apprehensive about it, she gave me a look of real sympathy. HUD, or Housing and Urban Development, is a government program for helping low-come people like myself afford their rent. While I was grateful for the rent subsidy, I very much resented the fact that this government program dictated to me where I could live, how I could live, and who I could live with. Now with the Prochlorperazine in my system, I had lingering doubts if I would be strong enough physically to be able to clean and tidy my place up so it would be presentable when the HUD Inspector arrived. He was to come and look over my apartment on July 8th. I was anxious. Even though most of it was now routine, making out the paperwork in my chemo-burdened condition had been task enough.

When I related all these apprehensions and misgivings, Chris showed that she was a friend who understood my feelings, as peculiar as they may have been. She offered to help me both physically and spiritually.

"If your HUD inspection is on the 8th, would you like me to come over to your place on the 7th and help with the cleaning?" she said with a kind smile.

"I could come and help too," chimed in Debbie.

"I might need for you guys to do that. This latest anti-nausea medicine has just about knocked me flat on my back," I said, feeling truly and thoroughly drained.

"I'm sorry you feel so lousy, but it'll pass," Chris continued. "Praying always helps bring strength. Would you like me to pray over you now?"

"Sure, I would like that very much, Chris," I told her as she and her daughter joined in a prayer for my health and well-being. I added my own requests to the Almighty for their and my own health and well-being.

Chris was actually able to pray while keeping her eyes on the traffic. I admired her for that. When our prayer was done, I continued lamenting about my housing situation, while Chris and Debbie listened.

"I truly wish that I could have a place of my own, one I wouldn't have to pay rent on. One I wouldn't need to be beholden to HUD for," I said in a voice full of sad tiredness.

"Try not to worry about that and never forget that God can step in and help you get a place of your own. My advice to you, April, is keep talking with God. Talk with him the way you would talk with your real father" As Chris said this, she gave me a smile, though her eyes revealed how serious she was feeling for me.

"Maybe God can help me market more books. If my books can sell enough, the first thing I'll do with the money is buy a house," I said, feeling somehow stronger from her prayer and words of encouragement. I knew that she was right.

In reply, Chris gave me a nod and returned her attention to her driving. Then she changed the subject.

"April, we're still in The Dalles. Is there a store you'd like to go to?" Chris asked.

"No, but thank you, anyway," I answered tiredly. I had some places I needed to go back in Goldendale, but not until I was back in my hometown. I fell asleep as Chris and Debbie began talking about some local guys they happened to be dating.

When we returned to Goldendale, I did a couple of short errands. When that was done, my driver dropped me off at my apartment complex.

"You're a strong woman!" she told me as I gave my "goodbyes" to her and her daughter.

"Thank you," I replied graciously, although I was thinking, *Hell yeah, I'm strong because I have to be. There's nobody to do my errands or look after me when I'm feeling the worst and just want to crawl away and sleep. Damn it!*

Although I had enjoyed my journey and prayer session with Chris, I decided to ride with my sister-in-law for my next appointment. This was because Cindy wanted to take me to her favorite pizza place in The Dalles, just her and me together. That was doable since, as a sweet tidbit of luck coming my way, she would stay behind in Goldendale, while my brother went to Michigan to attend a family reunion. Cindy was never much into travel and was now more of a homebody than anything. We would be nice company for each other.

I spent the rest of that day of my fourth appointment sleeping and working on my diary. That Prochlorperazine was in my system and would be for awhile. Still, I got a lot of journeling done. On the upside, I wouldn't be constipated nor nauseous. To quote C. S. Lewis, author of *The Lion, The Witch, and The Wardrobe*, I slept like a trout. Unfortunately, because of the Prochlorperazine, that's about all I'd feel like doing for the next week or more. Of course, I pushed myself to take Pepper for her walks, work for Mr. Peterson, and do the necessary errands. But my ambition to do my own house work was nil.

True to her word, Chris was a godsend. She and Debbie came over to my place on July 7th and helped me clean it from top to bottom. This had not really been necessary for my HUD inspection to go well since that department is more concerned with safety and having everything be in tip top shape than with neatness or even cleanliness. For instance, having the stove and smoke alarms working mattered more than if there was dirt on the floor. Still, I felt better that my apartment was neat and tidy when the Inspector came July 8th. Thankfully, the inspection went well and I was told that I qualified for another Section 8 housing rent discount for another year.

But in spite of that major victory, I was still feeling despondent. Even Billy and his puppets were only a cold comfort. While it was true that this latest anti-nausea drug does have some strong psychological effects — it is also prescribed for keeping schizophrenia under control – I could not, in all honesty, blame my mental malaise on this medication entirely. I had, as a root foundation from childhood, strong feelings of not just low self esteem, but actual self loathing. These feelings derived from the mistakes I made daily in trying to understand other people and trying to get them to understand me. Then too, I could be absent minded, slow thinking, and unfocused, with a tendency to make verbal mistakes like saying "hat" when I meant to say "cat". Throughout my life I would punish myself for doing absent minded things, like misplacing an item. This punishment consisted of self-harm, mainly using my right hand to hit my left wrist *hard.* Of course, these raps and slaps would not prevent me from making absent minded mistakes in the future, but they did provide temporary relief for my anger. The resentment that was directed against myself.

I was also feeling low because my book sales were not bringing in enough money for me to pull myself up out of Social Security and SSI(Supplemental Security Income). How I hated being on the government dole. It made me feel like I was being wasted as a person and as far as my talents were concerned. I felt I deserved better, that anyone in my position deserved better. But I couldn't see any way out of my government dole dependency. So I was plunged into a new cycle of despair.

In my dreams, Billy decided that I needed stronger medicine. On the fourth night following my fourth chemo treatment, he and his puppets brought in another key figure from Yakama myth and legend – the Williamette Meteorite. Known and long reverenced by his people as Tomanowos, Visitor From The Sky, this six and a half foot, 32,000 pound arc from Heaven is made of a nickel-iron alloy and pocked with many sharp-edged holes. I was familiar with this Tomanowos because I had studied it during my delving into the Indian legends of the Pacific Northwest. But I had also perused its engrossing geological history as well. This meteor had its origins in a clump of space debris called a planetesimal. This being a loose clump of rocks, gases, and other matter that astrogeologists conjecture are what actual planets are made from. Some force had loosed it from its nest of crude matter and sent it racing toward earth. It had landed in Montana and then, ages later, was swept along by melting glaciers until it was deposited in the area of the town of West Linn, Oregon, which is two miles from Oregon City. A sure inspiring story of strength and survival if ever there was one.

In this dream sequence where Billy brought me to Tomanowos face-to-face, he invited me to touch it freely. As I ran my fingers over it's rough, pitted surface, I felt the sheer magnetism of the celestial-borne rock. I snickered as I thought how the thing, with its nickel-iron composition, must have driven the compasses of the white men who first saw it, crazy. But therein lay some of its power. Touching the meteorite and listening to Billy and his puppets tell its remarkable story, made me feel grounded and more positive inside. Like my life mattered after all.

"Meteorites are gifts from the Great Spirit, April. They are sent to remind us of His ability to give us gifts of all kinds, including guidance and wisdom, but also material prosperity. Through Tomanowos, He is telling you to not despair, that He has already intervened on your behalf big time by making your tumors go away. But He is going to do more benefits for you. Just be brave and strong and keep believing in Him," counseled my friend.

"One thing I won't do is ever give up," I promised with a light-hearted laugh as I reached inside one of the meteorite's cratered holes and felt added strength by doing so.

After several more dreams involving Tomanowos and its healing medicine, my mental malaise lifted completely and I was ready to face my next and fifth Shaxu appointment with renewed positive hopes and determination to get better.

The days and weeks leading up to that July 23rd appointment were, however, the same old routine punctuated by special and momentous interludes. I wore my wig when I went anywhere, but mostly one of my turbans when I was home alone with Pepper. Often when I was hidden away in my apartment, I would simply go around with my head bare-naked. I would never go outside my door that way though. I took care of Pepper, my apartment, and myself, while taking out time to exercise at the gym, sew, work for Mr. Peterson, and work on my journal that I would some day turn into a memoir. I had finished my Irish historical novel and it was being published. It would be on the shelves soon.

A week after my fourth chemo treatment, during a dream of Billy, his puppets, and the portentous meteorite, Tomanowos, I felt a sudden reassurance, mixed with compassion, that there were many other cancer sufferers out there who were a lot worse off than I was. The morning following that nocturnal voyage, I met up with an acquaintance I hadn't seen in a while. Her name was Tammy and she was a down and out artist and poet of sorts. I met her and her man, Jerry, outside of one of the town's beauty parlors and learned that she had skin cancer. Worse yet, she had taken treatment for it, but now, it was back and more aggressive than ever. Worst of all, it was all over her body.

"I got this because I sunbathed too much when I was younger," she told me in a sadder but wiser tone.

I gave her my sympathies and promised to pray for her, but that was about all I could have done. I promised to keep in touch.

Days later, during a dog walk, I heard a woman's voice call me over to a white truck near the local MacKerron's Hardware Store on Main Street. When I followed the direction of the voice, I recognized the woman at once. She was Mary Ann, another acquaintance of mine. This lady once had a farm of her own and had sold fresh produce to market outside The Dalles. Now that her husband had left her, she had been forced to sell her farm, and now was living in Goldendale where she had moved to be close to family. Certainly, her mother, Jean, lived in that high prairie town and I knew her well. After all,

Jean was married to my nephew, Peter. Of course, Jean and Peter did everything they could to help Mary Ann with her financial and loneliness burdens, but now something worse had been added.

"I have two cancerous tumors, big ones, on my liver," Mary Ann remarked sorrowfully as I stood near her commiserating. I didn't say it out loud, but I was thinking, *Oh, my God, she has the black star. More than one, actually, horror of horrors!*

Keeping these dire thoughts to myself, I tried to tell her to trust the doctors she was working with. That a lot of medical miracles are possible today that weren't possible just a few years ago. We talked in that vein for several minutes, then Pepper started to tug impatiently on her leash. I gave her some final words of hope and then left the unfortunate black star victim, promising to keep her in my prayers.

Later on that evening, I thought to myself that Tammy and Mary Ann were, at least as I saw it, a lot worse off than I was. As dolorous as breast cancer is, I was glad I had that instead of what either one of those two women had in the way of cancer. As it was, my cancer had appeared to have already shrunk and then disappeared altogether.

But in my view, even if it hadn't, I would have still been better off. From my own perspective, I could literally keep my breast tumors hidden from view. And if worse came to worst, and one or both of my breasts had to be removed, I would forbearingly stuff cotton in my bra and deal with it. But with skin cancer, how can you hide that if it's on parts of your body that are out in public view? What can you do? Tammy's case was especially sad since a lot of it was on her face!

As for Mary Ann, she had the black star. That diagnosis was foreboding not only because liver cancer has an even higher death rate than breast cancer, but because that was what killed David Bowie, a rock star who always was, and always will be, a great musical and artistic inspiration to me. His death in 2016 was a great shock to me and to the world.

As my friend and neighbor, Julie, said to me, "I think his cancer death broke the universe a bit."

I prayed that Mary Ann wouldn't die of her black stars like he died of his. I hoped they could be removed and she could be given something, possibly radiation therapy, that would rid her whole system of cancer. In the meantime, I would keep in touch with her with cards and encouraging words.

A person who was a true comfort to me right then was my friend and neighbor, Marvin (Marvy) Dell. He was a computer buff who was really quite good at working with the gadgets and lived one trailer and one house away from me down the sidewalk on the left with his short-haired dog, Krissy. At sixty-five, he had his own health issues, but was always there to encourage me during my cancer trials and tribulations. As an added plus, he always had time to help me with any computer issues I might happen to have. Marvy, who was bald, bearded, and of average middle height and weight was no longer handsome. Perhaps he had never been what would be considered a "charmer", but he made up for it with his kind, gentle nature and loyalty as a friend. He told me that I was still pretty as well as huggable and squeezable even though I had no money and I had no hair, to roughly quote David Bowie in "Ashes To Ashes." He wasn't the only one who reassured me about my looks which made me feel a lot less like my whole life had been turned into smoldering ashes by the cancer and its attendant harsh chemical treatment.

Along with computer care and compliments, Marvy also brought me some cannabis tincture which really helped with my stomach aches. Although some people judge the products of that plant to be evil no matter what a person's needs might be, time and time again, it's been proven that oils from it will lessen and sometimes even take away, the stomach turning affects of chemo therapy. Lots of cancer patient's swear by it and I was proud to join their number. However, I stopped using cannabis tincture when I went off chemo and never took up the use of it again. I knew Marvy, crusty old hippy that he was, smoked weed a lot, but who was I to judge such a gentle soul. Everyone is entitled to a few vices.

On the evening of July 12th Marvy brought me a documentary of the Apollo Moon Landing of 1969 on a thumb drive. I watched it that evening with him and then watched it by myself for several evenings afterward. Viewing it got my mind off the cancer, the chemo, and Pepper's aging, the latter involving her teeth going bad. The engaging newsreel, which was very detailed, showed not just the voyage to the moon but the events and behind the scenes work that led up to it. It presented what was going on with the audience watching the initial fiery take-off, scenes in the control room at mission control, along with what Armstrong and the others were doing daily as they rode the gravitational pull of first the Earth then the Moon and visa versa for the flight back home. When they landed and walked out on the powdery lunar surface, the geologist in me became intrigued when Armstrong picked up and pocketed a lunar rock, a true "moon stone". After first seeing the film I couldn't resist looking up pictures and descriptions of the rocks and soil that the moon had offered up to be taken as "samples".

Yes, Marvy was the best friend ever and one of the people who helped me through this harsh time of my life. It was a huge plus that Krissy and Pepper got along well. We both enjoyed watching them play together like puppies near the steps of Marvy's big old white house.

My brother, Robert, also continued to be the loving support I needed and craved. Then on the 14th of July he really outdid himself. The Wednesday previous, he had invited me to go out with him for ice cream. I had declined, as I was feeling tired and unwell and said that probably by Sunday I would feel more up to enjoying such a jaunt. We both agreed to take a rain check. When the 14th which happened to be a Sunday rolled around, I got in touch with my brother again and he said he'd do it. Our get-together for ice cream was a sure thing.

"But I have to take my granddaughter Kelly out swimming first. Then I'll pick you up for ice cream," he promised.

"Hope you both have a great time at the local pool," I told him, all the while thinking of how the pool they were going to stood right beside the home I used to share with Ozzy.

I also thought, somewhat bitterly, of all the times I had attempted to learn to swim and had failed because of my dire lack of coordination. Swimming was another joyful activity that my disability had denied me for a whole lifetime. But I didn't share these sorrows with Robert during that brief phone interlude. I didn't need too. He was already aware of them. After he said "goodbye" and hung up, I spent my time journaling and sewing. I was working on a very tiny doll that I had neglected doing any work on because of other activities. It seemed that I waited hours for my brother to call again. Finally, he did and said he'd be over to get me in twenty minutes. Happy and feeling as light as a puppy on the first day of spring, I took Pepper for a walk and then got ready to go on my sibling date. In due time, Robert was there in his nice shiny gray car with its Search And Rescue license plate. He phoned, telling me that he was in the back parking lot and so I replied telling him that I'd be right there and hopped down the stairs. I left Pepper with a treat and with the TV on the ME channel.

Before driving me to MacDonald's, Robert parked the car momentarily and gave me some gifts. These were a necklace with a turtle-shaped pendant and a very nice tan-colored hat. Turtles were another animal that I looked to for strength at that time. Slow and plodding, they are still able to get the job done, whatever it happens to be. I admire that quality and cultivate it in myself. I also feel stronger by thinking of their shells as representing strength and protection – mental and emotional as well as physical. Of course, I liked to extend this idea to the concept of a shell of some kind protecting me from cancer. I didn't share any of these inner musings with my brother at that time, however. Instead, I just gave him a big hug and told him "thank you"!

"I don't celebrate birthdays, but we can still give each other gifts and have fun get-togethers," he said cheerfully.

"Of course," I told him happily. I didn't really agree with his religious objections to observing birthdays, but I was so happy to be on an outing with him I didn't care.

"Kelly got bored at the pool after being there for half an hour. Probably, because there wasn't anybody there that she knew. So I just decided to take her back home," Robert confessed.

"Did she enjoy being there at the pool at all?" I asked, trying to sound interested.

"Yes, but she soon tired of it and wanted to go home and watch movies and play games on her smartphone."

"Kids nowadays. They would rather play with their technology than go for a swim or a hike anyway."

"Not like when I was a kid. I loved being outdoors with my friends, goofin' around."

"When I was a kid in Canada, I would hike up in the mountains every day with my dog. It was really fascinating to me to go up in the highest peak and watch the weather being made. We were up that high."

"Kids now would rather watch celebrities do goofy things on their smart phones. Times have sure changed."

"Yes, they have. But Kelly's a good kid."

"Yes, she is."

In minutes, we were at MacDonald's and the golden arches welcomed us inside. I ordered a plain vanilla cone, while Robert ordered a chocolate fudge sundae. It would be awhile before I would feel up to enjoying a treat with a lot of garnishes. Robert got our ice cream and then led me over to seats by a window. It was a sunny, cheerful day outside with the wind not blowing too heavily. As we started eating our ice cream, I noticed that my brother had a knife with a lot of attachments. It was almost like a Swiss Army knife, but it didn't have quite *that* many attachments. Robert used the scissors part of it to cut open a packet of ground peanuts that were part of the topping of his ice cream treat.

"That's quite a clever knife, Robby, it must be a Swiss knife," I remarked.

"No, it's not got that many tools in it, but it's handy to have if you're deep in the woods," said my brother proudly as he showed me the rest of the knife's attachments and then returned it to his pocket. Besides the tiny scissors, it had two kinds of screw drivers, a knife, and a file.

"Remember Dennis Monroe?" my brother asked as he went to work on his sundae. The name did sound familiar, though I was unable to put a face to it.

"Yes, he was a family friend," I answered, as I felt old memories start to creep back.

"I went to high school with him and he was one of the guys I used to goof around with. You were very young at the time. So you probably wouldn't remember him much. But right after high school, he went into the marines. I remember him getting stationed in Japan."

At the mention of Japan, Robert really had my attention since I have always been fond of Asian countries. Feeling truly caught up in his discourse, I said nothing as I licked the smooth sweetness of my vanilla cone while he continued.

"After Dennis was stationed in Japan, in Okinawa, as I recall, he sent me and your sister some gifts. Remember the doll he sent to Delane? She gave it to mama and then she gave it to you. Do you still have it?" he inquired as he savored some chocolate topping.

"I do," I answered him beaming. "Lovely thing. I have her in my doll cabinet now."

As I said this, I thought with pride how that Japanese doll was indeed a gorgeous addition to the huge doll collection I had amassed over the years. "She" was thirteen inches tall and done in the elegant dress and lacquered hair style of a traditional geisha dancer – red brocade kimono, dangly silver hair piece, and all. Because my sister had given this cloth fan dancer to my mother and then my mother had given her to me, she was like a precious heirloom handed down in an inheritance.

"So, what did Dennis send you?" I continued, eager to know.

"He sent me a wooden Japanese puzzle box and a genuine Swiss knife with all the features."

"Wow that knife must have given you a lot of fun times whittling and doing handy repair jobs. Do you have it now?"

"No. *sigh*. I lost it when I moved to Canada in the 70s."

I was familiar those exotic puzzle boxes and had once had a fine collection of cheaper card board and paper versions of them. The Japanese versions, were called himitsu-bako, and like their Chinese counterparts appeared to have only one opening but really had three or more false ones to mislead the person who was attempting to open it.

"How about the puzzle box? Do you still have that?" I asked, trying to sound blithe as I started crunching on my cone.

"*Ha ha*. Yes I do, as a matter of fact, and it's still a challenge for me to open it," said Robert as he finished the last of his sundae.

"I remember getting one of those puzzle boxes as a prize at that fairgrounds the folks and I used to live close to in Hastings, Michigan. There was a fair there every late summer," I added with dreamy nostalgia.

"Yes, they gave away all kinds of knickknacks as prizes for dunking a floating duck or throwing a hoop over a pole on a board."

"*Ha ha*. I really enjoyed that dunk the duck one."

"My favorite thing to do there was just goof around with Dennis. I recall the day that somebody parked his car by our dad's refrigeration repair shop which was down the hill from our house and close to the fair grounds and all of its hoopla. Because the chevy was where it wasn't supposed to be, trespassing really, me and Dennis decided to play a little trick on the owner. We went under his hood and tinkered with the car's wires so it wouldn't run. When the man came back we hid and watched, while laughing under our breath as he became more and more frustrated trying to get his chevy to start. Finally after figuring out what was wrong and putting the wires back where they belonged, he got his car started and was on his way, with a lot of fussing and fuming that he would like to *beat to a pulp* whoever had messed with his car. Safe in our hiding place, Dennis and I never laughed so hard before in all our lives."

"Well, that was naughty. But really the guy had it coming and that is a really funny story. Thank you for giving me my laugh for the day, along with the ice cream. *Ha ha ha!*"

"Glad to oblige."

I finished crunching down the last of my cone and then we left the golden arches for my apartment.

"I really enjoyed our day together, April. We'll have to do it again sometime soon," said my brother as he dropped me off at my door.

"We will. I feel great today, in spite of that chemo, because you've made my day."

"I just hope I won't have to go through it myself."

"I will pray that you never do. I wouldn't wish this on anyone. Especially not someone I love."

Dismissing that brief shadow, I touched his hand in a comforting way. Then after giving him a hug, l left his car for my apartment where Pepper would be waiting for me with her little stub of tail twitching.

I walked her and then spent the rest of the day sewing on the tiny doll and doing research about puzzle boxes. I dreaded the next day, which would be a Monday. I was scheduled to take Pepper to the downtown animal clinic at 8:30 that morning. As, Paul Williams, another one of my musical and artistic influencers would sing, "Rainy days and Mondays always get me down".

Early the next morning and true to that somewhat gloomily romantic song's lyrics, it was indeed raining – hard! So I did the only thing that I could do. I put raincoats on me and Pepper, slipped on my pink wellingtons, and went out to brave the walk from my apartment to the veterinary office. As the raindrops splattered down and the puddles swelled, I thought to myself how nature herself seemed to be adding insult to my injury. I never did care much for so-called Mother Nature and her whimsies. All my life I wished I could have been a scientist-inventor capable of repealing every law Nature ever devised. Even gravity? Especially the law of gravity. It disappointed me that by that time, the year 2019, there still weren't such things as air cars that needed neither wheels nor highways. I pushed such disgruntled thoughts from my mind and forded the drizzly way to the vet's office, dodging traffic as well as rain puddles, some of which now seemed like small lakes. Indeed, a lot of them were starting to run together.

When Pepper and I reached the door of the veterinary clinic, both of us were soaking wet in spite of our rain gear. I checked her in and hoped to stay with her through whatever procedures the animal doctor would recommend, be they tooth extractions or just a thorough mouth cleaning. Unfortunately, I was informed that I would be forced to leave my dog at the clinic and go about some other errands and then go home without her since it would be two hours or more before the veterinarian could even look in her mouth. This was because there happened to be so many other animal patients in ahead of her. So I

114

gave Pepper a hug and told her to be brave for mommy. Sadly, I pulled the hood of my pink raincoat up over my head and went out to face the downpour.

First, I went to the post office and then afterwards bought a few items at the nearest grocery store. Because the bag they gave me to carry my purchases in was paper instead of plastic it started to fall apart on the way back to my apartment. Luckily, it held together well enough for me not to lose any groceries on the rain-soaked sidewalk.

Finally, I was trudging through the rain to the door of my apartment complex and the comparative warmth and comfort that lay within. By that time, I was softly crying, for the absence of my beloved pooch and for having exhausted myself in the cold and damp. Still, I made it up the stairs and unlocked my door where the doll I had made with my hair stood dangling as an almost welcoming sight. Once in, I put away the groceries, got on some dry clothes, and called the veterinary clinic. As a lucky break, I got the vet herself. She told me that Pepper would need to have some teeth pulled. I told her to pull as many as she needed too and that I would be waiting for further calls from her as my dog's treatment progressed.

She told me that she would keep in touch. On that note, I thanked her and then went to sleep for a whole hour. I was that wiped out.

Hours later, I heard from the vet again. She explained that because of the amount of teeth she had been forced to pull from her little mouth, thirteen in all, she felt it was best she keep Pepper overnight. Especially since she was still groggy from all the sedation she had needed to give her. Poor little Pepper. Of course, I was reluctant to leave my dog at the clinic, but wanted to do what was best for her. The vet kindly assured me that she thought it was best that Pepper stay where she was until morning. I thanked her and then let her go. My night without the love and comfort of my canine companion was a rough one. Still, I made it through until morning. I was too distraught to go to gym, however. At 8:00 am, I phoned the animal clinic to find out how my dog was doing. The girl at the desk could not give me any news, but said she would have the vet call me about Pepper. So reluctantly I thanked her and then ate an uneasy breakfast which I followed up with a fitful short nap. In the middle of it, the vet phoned.

"She's still quite drowsy, but you can come and get her," she informed me. I told her cheerfully that I'd be right over.

Luckily it wasn't raining and the wind wasn't blowing a gale either. So I was able to hurry to the clinic with Pepper's leash. When I got there, the vet led me to one of the examination rooms where I noticed that my doggie did indeed seem a bit dopey and a little out of it. Even so, she recognized me and came over and licked my leg. I leaned down and scooped her up in my arms. She licked my cheek. The vet gave me some pills for her to take, antibiotics they were, and then offered to have someone drive me and her back home. I declined, saying that a walk would be good for both of us. The animal doctor then noticed my hair and said it looked nice. I thanked her, but told her that it wasn't real, that I was forced to wear a wig because I was going through cancer treatments. Her reaction was one of sympathy and not alarm. She repeated again her offer to give me and my dog a ride home. Wishing to avoid mud puddles with my dog who was still a bit wobbly on her feet, I agreed for the vet to drive us back to my apartment.

After a final "thank you", I paid the receptionist twenty dollars and was out the door. The kind animal doctor took the driver's seat while I loaded Pepper into the seat beside her and climbed in myself. As I rode home, I looked out my window and noticed how bright and sunny it was with green leaves and summer flowers everywhere. It was going to be a happy day. Pepper and I were back together again and she would be healthier with all those bad teeth gone. I made a promise to myself that from then on, I would have her teeth professionally checked and cleaned once each year.

That night I had a dream that was enjoyable and also mildly full of portent. In it, I found a salmon skeleton thermometer, two Indian dolls, and a bracelet of wooden and baked clay beads – all items I'd had as a little girl, but thought I'd lost or misplaced. In the weeks that followed that dream, I found all of these items packed away in boxes I'd forgotten about.

"The lesson here," Billy explained from his place near the packing crates. "Is that what is valued and lost will always return to you. If not in this world, then in the next."

This revelation filled me with hope to face whatever outcomes of my cancer treatments might be around the corner.

DISASTER EIGHT

On the day of my fifth treatment, I woke up at 5 am and took Pepper out. It was a lovely morning. The sun wasn't completely up, but the day was already warm. I was feeling nervous, but braced for the day. I was gearing up to confront the nurses about various subjects pertaining to my treatment that day. The main issue was I didn't want my arm bound to a board. I had talked it over with my niece twice and she told me I didn't need to put up with that sort of what was for me unnecessary restraint.

"Just tell the nurse you don't want to be restricted that way and that she has to trust you not to pull the tube loose," said Katie strongly, but with great sympathy.

I thanked her for her support and encouragement and after our phone call felt stronger. For the rest of the evening I gave myself pep talks where I said out loud what I planned to say to the nurses.

"No more boards on the arm!"

I also had other things I needed to mention. I made a list.

During my walk with Pepper, I ran into my neighbor Andy and his dog. He would be looking after Pepper the whole time I was in The Dalles. We talked a bit, mostly about my treatment and about his blood sugar problems.

"Don't worry, April. I'll look after Pepper for you. I'll take her for a walk at 11:00 am. And you don't need to pay me anything. I'm just doing what neighbors do. We help each other. I know that you would do the same for me if my dog needed someone to look after him," said Andy as he pointed at his little Skippy dog.

Andy has the broadest, most heavily muscled arms that I find very attractive. Another feature in his favor, in my eyes, is his short stature. I have always adored short men. My own father was only 5 feet 6 inches. But it's his patient, open-hearted nature that is the most appealing, plus his loving way with dogs.

"I sure would look after your Skippy. I'd be my pleasure. I will be back by 2:00, but if I can't make it back by then, I'll phone you," after giving my friend that last promise, I gave him a hug and returned with Pepper to my apartment. I did a few chores – folding clothes, washing dishes, and scrubbing the kitchen floor. In between these activities, I would stop and give my dog a pat on the head or a scratch on her back or behind her ears.

Before I knew it, my phone rang. On the other end was my sister-in-law telling me that she was waiting for me in the back parking lot. It was time for me to go.

"I'll be down in a second," I told her quickly.

Then I turned on ME-TV for the dog, checked my purse to make sure I had packed my keys, and was down the stairs and out the door like a bunny rabbit. Incidentally, "Bunny" was a nickname I had received in early childhood but had since outgrown. It hadn't helped that I had been born on Easter Day.

Once outside I walked quickly over to my sister-in-law's gray Toyota and got in. We were both glad to see each other and said "hi." Then we were on our way. We talked as we sped

119

past dry hills crowned with slowly revolving wind turbines. They resembled in the morning sun knights in white armor standing guard with white lances over the hills of Gresham, their king's realm. Their massive rotating spears seemed to point us in the direction toward The Dalles as we circled the hills they flanked. As I watched them, I thought of the days before these mighty sentinels were erected. Ozzy would take me on car trips to visit such hills that were even further outside of the city. During these journeys, when these slopes and valleys were still occupied only by wild flowers and grassy nooks for viewing the craggy mountains above and the waters of the Columbia River below, Ozzy and I would go for walks with a Schnauzer or two tagging along behind. Usually, these walks would end in a picnic in the sun and breeze. Then I would gather wildflowers to sketch and write poems about. He and I would spend whole days like that, just enjoying the countryside unadorned by the devices of mankind. In all truth, as much as I admired the towering beauty of the wind turbines, a large part of me missed the days when I walked hand in hand with Ozzy under a sky that didn't have them. More than that, I missed holding hands with him. A tear trickled down my cheek. Then I returned my attention to Cindy who was wrapped up in her driving, seemingly lost in her own thoughts.

Soon, the wind turbines came to a halt and I began to see instead rocky hills which were lined with crevices from which green grass patches sprouted. Occasionally, I would see small herds of cattle grazing there. Below these cattle were a blooming daisy-like plant called the wild sunflower. I pointed them out to my sister-in-law.

"Aren't those yellow flowers with the brown centers lovely. They're called wild sunflowers and I like to draw them and write poems about them," I said, suddenly more cheerful.

"I know you do. Robert and I have cards you made for us full of sketches of those flowers and poems and short stories you wrote about them," said Cindy as she briefly cast her gray-blue eyes on a road bank loaded with the bright blossoms.

"Making those cards was fun. One of my main pleasures in life," I answered wistfully, thinking of the sad fact that I had let my card-making for friends and family slip ever since I had gotten caught up in my war with cancer.

Even so, I had made a special card for my brother, one depicting a Schnauzer dog driving a Model T Ford, just three weeks ago. I resolved to make a special card for Cindy too. Possibly one with a bouquet of wild sunflowers sketched on it.

We went past huge square stone formations, many of which were broken here and there by hollows full of grass and small trees. Some had seasonal brooks rushing by at their bases. Then we sped past flat land with sparse grass and bushes and came across the bridge that divided Oregon from Washington. As we crossed it, I looked down on the rocks and saw not only seagulls, but pelicans.

"I see pelicans!" I nearly exclaimed to Cindy, while inside I remembered a nonsense rhyme that my father had been particularly fond of.

"A remarkable bird is the pelican,
His beak can hold more than his belly can."

I thought then of my short statured Irish father who had passed away in 2005 in a veterans' nursing home in The Dalles. Before being placed in there by my brother, he had lived in a comfy little house situated in the middle of a small Canadian village called Midway. Some of my happiest days were those spent while visiting him there with Ozzy and our dogs. Just then Cindy cut into my somewhat melancholy reverie.

"Yes, I never used to see them out on those boulders. Just seagulls. Now I see those birds out there crowding out the seagulls," she remarked with a chuckle.

"They're competing for fish," I answered as I continued to focus on the big-beaked birds. Indeed, there did seem to be more of them than the usual rock perchers.

"I'm sure they are and I heard that the river is full of fish right now," Cindy added as we rode all the way across the bridge, past the huge *River's Edge Health & Wellness Center* hospital, and up the hill to the right where the bulk of the small city's medical facilities were.

"Where did you hear that from?" I asked as I stared up at the grassy escarpment on the edge of town where a line of simple houses stood.

"From an old Indian fisherman who goes to our Hall. I believe his name is Billy," said Cindy in a wistful voice.

I turned my gaze over to her and smiled. Greatly comforted by the coincidence in names though I said nothing. Just then we were in the Shaxu parking lot. We left the air conditioned car and stepped into a pleasantly balmy day. The sky above was mostly a powder blue though there were thunderheads in the distance.

"Well here we are, April. Ready for your big adventure. Remember this is your next to the last treatment," said Cindy as she flipped her car beeper which told us every door was locked.

"Thanks for telling me that. It makes me feel better," I said as I picked up my pace to walk beside her.

While I wasn't looking forward to the confrontations I was expecting with the nurses, I was resolved to be strong and determined, though still nice about the whole thing involving my desire not to be strapped to a board. As I walked past the tranquil man-made pool that spanned the walkway, I rehearsed in my mind what I was going to say to them. I also looked for fish and scolded myself for expecting to find any in there. Sandy went ahead of me a couple paces and opened the double doors for me. Then we walked past the main building receptionists, said some brief "hellos!", and bolted up the steps to the infusion room reception area. I immediately checked in with the receptionists there and then joined Cindy as she made her way to the bathroom. I had drank my full 8-glass clear water quota that morning and was feeling like a sieve.

After us two girls had both relieved ourselves we went and took our places in the waiting room. I sat and read from *The Centerville Ghost.* Cindy sitting beside me looked at a book featuring lovely pictures of the forest and river-rich Pacific Northwest. Occasionally, I stole some glances over at those colorful photos, recognizing many local landmarks. I amused myself this way between the two books for a while and then who should appear on the scene than Stan the massage man, he of the warm, sweet smile, gentle blue eyes, and strong nimble fingers.

"Can I give you two ladies a back rub?" he asked as he cracked his limber knuckles.

"Not I," declined Sandy who said this without raising her eyes from the charming travel book.

"I'll take it," I said without hesitation. "But it's my neck that needs it the worst."

So, I sat in a comfy, straight-backed chair he provided and our session began.

"Please mostly do my upper back and neck," I said as I leaned back into the soothing feel of the padded chair back and Stan's ready fingers.

And he went right to work.

"Yes, April, you do have a lot of tension in your neck area, but I also feel it in your jawline. May I massage your jawline too?" he asked, his hands moving from my neck to my jawline and back again.

Already, I was starting to feel less pain, while Cindy looked up from her book now and then to regard us with a smile. He continued easing the tension generated pain in my upper back, my neck, and my jawline, while we talked about gardens. His strawberries had petered out, while he was up to his juice stained elbows in raspberries. I appreciated that since I had enjoyed raspberry patches on my farm when I was a kid in Canada. As we talked on in this vein and Stan's administrations continued, I began to forget all about my pain. It had its origins, no doubt, in my bad eyesight which was now causing me to bend over my work while I worked on my colored pencil sketches and my sewing. Unfortunately, my eyes aren't as good as they used to be. But all of that slipped into the background as Stan's fingers slipped over my tension spots and we talked about our individual experiences with picking raspberries. He also directed my attention to the gathering gloom outside the building's tall windows.

"The sky is blue enough now, but the way the dark clouds are creeping up this way, we could be in for some rain," Stan said softly.
"Oh, well," the flowers around here need it and so do your raspberries," I replied drowsily.

"Indeedy they do," he agreed as he tapped his fingers along the line of my upper spine.

Just as I was getting so comfortable I was starting to doze off, my name was called. The time of the dreaded blood draw had arrived. I went where I was directed too and to where I was to sit to have my veins opened. Thankfully the old biddy, Nurse Poule, wasn't there to do the honors. I should at this time, point out that in my mind the term "old biddy" has nothing to do with age or even gender. In my lexicon, even a twenty-year-old male, who's bossy, emotional, and fussy enough can be an old biddy.

Thankfully, my arm was instead sanitized and then poked by a nicer lady named Denise and her young assistant. Without any trouble, they hit the right vein in the hollow of my elbow pit and some blood was taken. They also set me up to receive my infusions. At that point, I mentioned that I didn't want my arm strapped to a board.

"You guys are just going to have to trust me not to get up and start moving my arm around like one of those white wind tur-bines," I said seriously, but with patient humor.

"That'll be up to you and your nurse," said Denise as she taped the infusion tube tighter in place. I gritted my teeth at the thought of needing to talk with that obnoxious practical nurse again. Then I put on my sweetest Aspartame grin and changed the subject.

"Please don't put me in a separate cubicle again. Being in one makes me freeze, so I'd rather be out with the general public," I said in voice oozing with fake sweetness.

"Of course, but I thought you wanted to be in a cubicle all by yourself," said the younger technician.

Where on earth did she get that idea? I thought briefly to my-self with a frown. Then I tipped it up into a put-on smile and continued.

"No thank you," I said in voice filled with sweetness but at the same time strong resolve.

"All right, we'll put you out in the main seating area".

"Thank you very much."

But when I reached the general seating area, another young nurse offered me a private cubicle. *Where do all of these idiots came from?* I wondered to myself with rising irritation. Quickly, I put on my sweet masks of both face and mood and declined.

"No thank you. I'll be happy to sit right here," I said, directing my hand to a chair.

Beside of it sat my sister-in-law smiling invitingly. She had brought my purse, along with the Pacific Northwest scenery book. But it wasn't time for me to take my infusions yet. I was to see Dr. Xiwang first, but before him, to my chagrin, I was to see Nurse Poule first. She weighed me, took my blood pressure, and listened to my heart while asking me what I thought were stupid questions about my weight as it related to my age. I had lost ten pounds, but I wasn't starving because of chemo-generated nausea. Still, she suspected so.

It was a great relief when she at last left and was replaced by Dr. Xiwang, my hero. After we greeted each other, he asked me how I was doing. I told him that I was doing better than I deserved, a quote I borrowed from a radio talk show host and financial adviser named Dave Ramsey. This bit of humorous whimsy caused a broad smile to crease his handsome face. His grin made my heart flutter happily. The man is very handsome and had taken me through so much during my treatments. I also found his back ground decidedly intriguing. He had been born in Northern China near the town of Yumen and been educated at China Medical University in Liaoning Province. When I asked him what had inspired him to take on a career in medicine, his answer was terse, but touched by a hint of pride.

"My parents. Both of them were physicians," he said with an engaging smile.

That was on the day of my third treatment. Now I was going to be put on my next to the last one. I was feeling better emotionally, almost optimistic. Cindy was still in the seat beside my soon-to-be infusion chair waiting for me while remaining engrossed in her book.

"Since the tumors appear to be gone from my breasts and armpits, what will my next course of treatments, if any, be," I asked in a voice full of cautious hope.

"I will have you put through a PET and CT scan and if your cancer is all clear, I'll put you on a hormone blocker and antibodies," he said as our meeting came to a close. I shook hands with him and thanked him.

As I left for the public infusion area, I was thinking to myself naively that the "antibodies" he mentioned would simply be antibiotics of some sort. I would learn the full medical truth soon enough. In the meantime, I had other things to concern me. Right there was the old biddy with her obnoxious arm board.

"No thank you, ma'am. I don't want to be put on an arm board. I consider it to be unnecessary as well as harsh and restraining," I told her as she and her younger assistant stood by waiting to hook me up to the IV.

"But if I don't the whole thing could come free and you could get badly burned by the infusion. I've seen people need skin grafts after burns like that," she said in a hands ringing tone

127

of voice that I found more irritating than anything the chemo could ever do to me.

I even had thoughts that what the practical nurse was saying might not even be true. That she was just using scare tactics to control. Still, I was polite but firm.

"No arm board, thank you," I insisted.

But I was not to be let off the hook by her so easily. Just as the assistant was preparing to put the first infusion bag in place, Nurse Poule left and returned again. She was looking highly agitated and was wringing her hands.

"April, the results of the blood tests show that you have a fatally high amount of potassium in your system and must report to MCMC next door to bring it, hopefully under control!" Nurse Poule exclaimed.

I was stunned, scarcely able to believe my ears.

"That serious! But I feel fine," I protested, feeling emotionally glued to my seat.

"It is that serious. It could wreak your heart," cautioned the old biddy who continued to wring her hands.

"Right now or in the long term?" I asked, feeling like I was caught up in nightmare.

"Right now! Your heart could stop right now!" the nurse practitioner nearly shouted.

"We really need to go to MCMC then, April. I can't have you croaking on me," added Cindy whose face and voice showed great concern.

Like a zombie I let myself be led over to MCMC to get my potassium under control. I must confess that I wasn't in the most agreeable mood. Later I would wonder why, if they thought I really was dying, wasn't I wheeled over there in a wheel chair?

Be that as it may, I made it over to the clinic and checked in, barely able to concentrate on what I was supposed to sign. Still I made it through, even signing a directive agreeing that I wanted to be revived if I went into cardiac arrest, all the while showing the staff my caustic mood through caustic remarks. I had been frightened and every emotion I had was rubbed raw.

"Of course I want to be revived. If I didn't want to live, I wouldn't be here!" I told the receptionist with barbed sarcasm.

In a moment, I was checked into an emergency room. My sister-in-law and I waited for what seemed like an hour.

"This doesn't make sense. If they thought you were going to die right away, why are they making you wait so long?" asked Cindy with pointed wisdom.

"I know that doctor visits are usually hurry up and wait, but this is ridiculous. Doesn't someone who's supposed to be on their last legs have priority?" I fumed.

Half an hour later, two technicians appeared. I have to confess that I wasn't too pleasant with them, but I was about at my wit's end.

"Hey, we just got here," was the defensive rebuttal of one of the ladies.

They had me strip and put on a hospital gown. Then they hooked me up to a heart monitor. Thankfully, my heart checked out healthy. Then they took some blood tests. This wouldn't have been so bad, but the technician doing it bruised me a couple of times while looking for a "good" vein. After taking enough blood samples, one of the technicians informed me of the dire outcome that might await me should a further testing of my blood reveal a potentially fatal level of potassium in my blood.

"If we can save you at all, you will have to spend the night here taking infusions of first glucose and then insulin. We will try to bring your potassium down, but we might not be able to. In which case you could die here tonight. But we have to try," announced the lab technician gravely.

"Insulin? But I'm not diabetic," was all I could say in stunned protest.

"We know you're not. That's why we are giving you glucose infusions before the insulin," she added with professional coldness.

Then she and the other woman left to do the dire tests. I looked at Cindy who was close to tears.

"Could you please stay the night?" I asked in a voice weak with emotion.

"Yes, if it comes to that," her words were reassuring although her voice was sad.

At that, both of us started praying harder than we'd ever prayed before. But it was hard to concentrate. In the next room was a teenager, who had gotten a serious alcohol overdose and was suffering withdrawal. How she screamed and cried. This racket caused me to feel worse, even more of a sense of dread about my own awful predicament.

Hours later, the technician was back with the lab results. I wasn't going to die or need to spend the night in that hospital with the screaming teenager. I apologized to the lab technicians for my formerly terse behavior and they both said it was okay, they were aware just how scared I was and it was only natural for me to act that way. What made the potassium scare even worse was that it had been the result of an error on the part of one of the lab technicians. I was furious, but kept my cool. Somehow I blamed that irksome Nurse Poule for the fiasco that would leave me traumatized for a good, long time.

I left MCMC feeling thoroughly rattled, but determined to do my chemo treatments even though the staff told me I could go home and schedule to do them four days later. It was 2:00 by that time, far later than usual, and I just wanted to take them and get them over with. Of course, I put on a brave, cordial front and submitted to being hooked up to the infusion machine.

After everything was in place for my first infusion bag and it was starting to go into me, Nurse Poule returned and had me lay my arm on a pillow. That was not so bad. It was my left arm and I could easily move my right arm to read, write, and even eat. But I found in time that if I moved my left arm or hand at all, the device bringing the medicine would shut down with a loud *beep!* and need to be restarted again. Worse still, the old biddy would have to come over and turn it back on again and would ask me if I'd moved my arm or hand in an increasingly irritable voice. At one point, my sister-in-law left the room to go for a walk since she was starting to get cramps in her lower back and tail bone. So, just to be ornery, I would tell the nurse that no I hadn't moved my left arm or hand at all. I did that a few times, but after Cindy returned, I felt compelled to be more honest, but still stand my ground. I didn't doubt that Nurse Poule was still trying to control me. And it was her job to put my infusion tube back in place. What on earth was

131

she being paid to do anyway?

"It taddle tales on you if you move even a little bit. So didn't budge," she reprimanded me sharply as she checked the infusion tube and then turned the machine back on.

I said nothing back, but determined that I would ask to have another nurse on my case next time. Still, I got by and got through my treatment. I even managed to eat a plate of cheese, crackers, and apples that I shared with Cindy. And I was able to write and read, just not as much as I would have liked to.

After the session was done, I was unhooked and I got a card from a receptionist nurse describing my next and last chemo appointment. Pleased that it would be on a Tuesday at ten instead of nine, I thanked her and then left the building. Outside, it was starting to look dark and foreboding out, but Cindy was hungry. And even though it went against every norm of medical science, so was I. So together we went to the MOD pizza place which was more than a little off-beat but served superb pizzas and milkshakes. She bought a double medium-sized pizza and small milkshakes for both of us. I call it double because one side of it had a filling that she liked, she likes lots of onions, while they don't agree with me. My side had lots of ham, tomatoes, olives, and spinach. As for the milkshakes, I ordered a vanilla one for Cindy and a chocolate one for me.

One of the things that made the place outre' was, besides the walls being studded by strange and exotic scenes from downtown Portland, was that you had the servers make your pizza with topping you chose. In that way it was very like Subway. Ingenious idea. Cindy and I took our places on stools in front of a large window. Outside, the encroaching storm clouds had massed into a threatening sheet of darker gunmetal gray. Even so, we took our time to enjoy our supper, while looking over the pictures above the sign on the wall that read, "Keep

MOD Weird". This was, of course, a paraphrase of the popular expression, "Keep Portland Weird". This saying always brought shivers of delight up and down my spine. As Cindy and I munched on our halves of the pizza and drained our milkshakes, we laughed together at some of the photos. One that particularly caught my eye was of the infamous Portland nude bicycle ride since it had a lot of well-built male riders. I was disappointed though that the photo didn't show as much of them as I would have liked to see. But, of course, any family restaurant, no matter how weird, has to have family-friendly décor.

We finished our meal and by that time, it was 5:00 pm. As we walked out to Cindy's car, we saw that lightning was starting to cut flashing streaks in the sky over the hills. We climbed in and were on our way back to Goldendale. On the whole way, it didn't rain. Even so, the lightening and the thunder became increasingly more startling. Cindy's biggest worry was that all that lightning, without rain, over the dry hills and plains could start fires.

"It's happened more than once near our place. I hope that all this dry lightning doesn't start a fire again," said Cindy who was very worried.

"I hope not too. It seems to be a pattern in this part of the country where first it gets very hot, then forest fires break out, then it usually rains," I said sharing my seasonal observation.

"Unfortunately, it doesn't usually rain enough to put the fires out once they get really started."

"Yes, that's when they have to bring in the fire work crews and the water planes."

We looked around and saw to our alarm that a good-sized island in the Columbia River had already caught fire and was burning drastically. The smoke was starting to make me sneeze.

"I'm just glad there are no people living there," said Cindy who was starting to feel the effects of the smoke herself. "They would have trouble leaving there if they didn't have a boat."

"Or a small plane," I added feeling a little apprehensive.

"Just as long as there isn't a fire up ahead near the highway. Looking at the smoke ahead, I'm afraid there might be," said Cindy as another streak of lightning pierced the sky overhead. Now I was really feeling apprehensive.

But as it turned out the next wave of smoke was coming from a brush fire far away from the main road. Still, it looked really scary and the smoke from it was thick in the air. I sneezed and Cindy did too.

Even so, we made it back to Goldendale safe and sound. A half hour after being dropped off at my apartment, I phoned Cindy to make sure she had returned safely to her house under the basalt cliffs and ponderosa pines.

"I got home, April. I'm a little tired but I'm fine," said Cindy cheerfully.

"I hope there aren't any fires close by your place," I mentioned with a slight feeling of unease.

"None, thank goodness."

"Yes, thank goodness for that."

After talking with her some more in a similar vein, I thanked her again for taking me to my appointment and wished her a goodnight.

"Please give my love to my brother and your dog, Henry," I added, feeling the shades of night drawing closely around me.

"Will do, April. Love you."

"Love you too, Cindy."

Soon after the phone call, I took Pepper out for her evening stroll. Then we went and thanked Andy for looking after her.

"Was she any trouble?" I asked him half-seriously.

"Not at all. It was my pleasure," he answered as he followed that up with a good bear hug.

That night, I watched my Babylon 5 science fiction show with my dog beside me. Following that, I bedded down with her and enjoyed a most wonderful dream. I drifted off to sleep feeling optimistic that night.

In this dreamscape, I met Billy as usual in the vacant lot where he had his packing crate theater.

"I bring you hope this night, something you need to nurture in your heart most of all," after saying this, he brought out the two puppets that resembled my brother and sister-in-law and did a song and dance skit the theme of which was that they loved me and that I should never give up hope of having a happy, fulfilling life.

When they were done, he put them away and pointed up at the sky. Instantly, I saw the tail of a meteor arc across the midnight black sky. Then to my vast surprise, not to mention alarm, the meteor started falling towards me. I recognized it at once. It was the Willamette Meteorite, old Tomanowos himself, though scaled down much, much smaller.

"Do not be afraid, April. It is a sign of hope for you. Hold out your hands and catch it," Billy commanded.

I did as I was told and soon I was holding in my two hands a miniature meteorite made of nickel and iron. Miraculously, it didn't burn me even though it was fresh from its journey through the heavens. As I held it, I truly felt love and hope run like electricity through my entire body. I kissed it.

"Here is another sign of hope for you, April," said Billy as he pointed up to the corner of the wall of the ruined building with a burning torch made of smudge sticks.

On that wall I became aware of something I just hadn't noticed before but should have. It was the ladder-like figure of a man done in pictograph form painted with reddish brown paint. Along with the flames from Billy's incense torch, the figure was brought into clear view by a beam of moonlight as though it were a special blessing from Heaven. A blessing especially for me.

"Note this picture and note it well. It is of an emissary from The Great Spirit, an angel. He will give you hope and strength when you need it the most," promised Billy.

I heard the sound of Indian drums pound in a steady beat that became progressively louder. Then the scent of the smudge sticks became thicker and heavier and Billy and his puppets were gone. I was still holding the palm-sized meteorite.

"Remember to always have hope, April," Billy's voice wafted gently, but forcefully on the incense-laden wind.

I slept peacefully and dreamlessly for the rest of the night and when I awoke the next morning, my heart and soul were brimful of hope. Also, from then on I would feel greater respect, along with comfort and strength every time I walked past the walls of the hollow where a burned down store had once stood, where Billy now put on puppet shows to give spirit to my dreams, and where my new hope-bringing guardian danced in all his brown splendor.

I now felt greater courage and self-worth. With this new awareness, it was easier for me to assert myself. The day following my fifth chemo treatment and the potassium scare, I stood up for my own self-worth by phoning Shaxu and asking them to replace Poule as my nurse. I also made a complaint against her, linking her to that mix-up in the lab which brought me so much consternation.

"Kimberly Jackson can be your nurse practitioner from now on instead of Anne Lynne Poule. I'm sure she would be a better fit for you, when it comes to personality and skills," said the girl at the desk kindly.

"Thank you, Miss. Poule and I just aren't compatible. Then there's that accident in the lab that nearly got me a frightening overnight stay at MCMC! I won't be able to forget that in a while," I said with strong emotions I was barely able to corral.

"I'm sorry that happened, Ms. Berrigan, but try not to worry. I will let Doctor Xiwang know about that and, trust me, he'll do something about it to make sure it never happens again," said the receptionist with great empathy.

"Thank you, give my love to my doctor," I said, feeling truly cheered.

"I will, Ms. Berrigan and take care. You are doing so well I hear," the receptionist responded with a laugh in her voice.

Even so, it was more like she was laughing with me than laughing at me.

"My cancer is gone, thank God" I said, finally feeling on top of the world and all of my problems.

"Yes, thank God. He does work in marvelous, mysterious ways, doesn't He, Ms. Berrigan?"

"Indeed, he does. Bye for now and see you when I come in for my next to the last chemo infusion."

"Bye, Ms. Berrigan."

"Bye and God bless."

DISASTER NINE

With my new guardian and surrounded by blooming wild sunflowers, my life went on. Even though I had some ups and downs with my stomach, especially at night, everything was going fairly smoothly, all things considered. I was still going to the gym and though my muscle strength had lessened due to the chemo treatments, I could still go strong with my weights and the benching bar. Every other day, I was doing hour long workouts. Pepper had gotten stronger on her back legs, although she was no longer up to the long walks we used to take. Although my acid reflux persisted, I was eating and keeping my food down. I had to be careful not to eat too much or at night, however.

I was sewing and happy with my writing projects. I made a couple of skirts and a very tiny Raggedy Ann doll. I sold that doll to someone who treasured it so much that she paid fifty dollars for it. This lady lives in a tall brown house in the residential section of town and is a longtime collector of Raggedy Ann and Raggedy Andy dolls. In fact, she has what amounts to a private museum of them and one of my joys is visiting her so I can see this display of these dolls which are of every size and shape. Some of them are very old. One Raggedy Ann was sewn back in 1915 but is still in remarkable shape.

Life was going well with summer in full swing. Then on July 25, I received a tremendous blow. I woke up at 5:00 am as usual and prepared for Pepper's walk. I was feeling weaker than usual and still half asleep, but I went through the routine well enough of feeding her and then putting on my clothes and shoes. But suddenly, I felt even weaker. So much so that I slipped to the kitchen floor and then fainted. Luckily, I had the presence of mind to check my fall so I wasn't hurt. I laid there unconscious for several minutes. When I got up I felt so weak that I had to go back to bed again. I was sorry about it, but Pepper's walk would have to wait. Just for the record, I had felt no weakness on either side and I wasn't in any pain. My heart area had no pain and I wasn't short of breath. I was just very weak.

At 9:00 am, I got up again and took her out while feeling so weak that it was hard for me to go down the stairs. But I made it. She did her business and then I led her through the apartment back parking lot. Then the tiredness hit me so hard that I went over to my neighbor Jed's police car and slumped on the hood of it. I guess I did that to feel more secure since it was a police car.

"April, are you all right?" called out Andy who had noticed me declining into my sorry state.

"No, I'm not!" I called back in as strong a voice as I could muster. At that point, I was barely able to keep my grip on the patrol car hood.

Andy and his dog came over and he peeled me off the hood. Then he carried me back to my apartment with Pepper under his strong arm and Skippy scampering close behind on his leash.

I spent the rest of the day feeling very weak. I did do a few chores though and some work on a blouse I was making. But mostly I slept. Understandably, I made arrangements with Andy to be my walking partner when I took Pepper for her 5:00 walk. I didn't want to be alone in case I felt weak again.

When 5:00 rolled around, I managed to make it down the stairs and join Andy and his dog at the door of his apartment. He supported me with his strong arms as I walked slowly down the stairs with Pepper close beside me. When I got to the bottom, I was exhausted, but kept on. My dog needed her walk. Andy and Skippy walked beside us as we made our way down the sidewalk near our apartment complex, across the street, and over to the sidewalk beside the willow-shaded funeral home.

At that moment I became so weak that I collapsed in Andy's arms. I didn't faint, I just crumpled down to my knees. Ever so gently, he eased me to the sidewalk. First, I lay there. Then I felt well enough to sit up. Even so, I was feeling even weaker than I had before. Pepper came over and nuzzled me with concern and sympathy.

"I'm going to call an ambulance, April," said Andy as he pulled his own dog in closer and brought out his smart phone.

"Go right ahead," I managed to gasp out.

Andy made the 911 call and then an ambulance came around the corner. I was still sitting on the sidewalk feeling completely drained. The care team took my vital signs. My blood pressure and heart beat were way below normal and sinking fast.

"You seem to be dehydrated, missy," said one of them, a muscular fellow with a broad mustache.

Urgently they loaded me into the vehicle and then I was on my way to emergency. En route, one of them took a blood test for diabetes.

"But I'm not diabetic," I protested.

"It's standard procedure that we still have to check you for it cause you nearly passed out," explained the other thinner man who was clean shaven and bald.

I gasped in some irritation. I knew that I wasn't diabetic. The man read my blood sugar number and was satisfied that I wasn't either. What a bothersome test!

Andy, who had no driver's license at the time, put both our dogs in his apartment and got a neighbor named Willy to drive him to the hospital behind the ambulance that was taking me. Soon we were through the emergency entrance. He helped me check in. The ambulance team put me in the care of some nurses and then left. Moments later, I was informed that I would need intravenous saline solutions. "For your dehydration," I was told. Just then, who should appear but my brother and sister-in-law, looking worried and fit to be tied. Andy had called them and explained what was happening. They all sat around as I was given the saline solution. And this on top of the infusions I had already received at Shaxu a couple of days earlier.

When that was done, a nurse took my blood pressure and heart rate. Both were getting closer to normal. Then a doctor informed me that I would need a plasma transfusion as well since I had checked out as drastically anemic.

"Your red blood cell count is so low, it could be fatal," he told me.

When the doctor told me that I would need a transfusion with blood plasma, Robert and Cindy looked at me questioningly. Their religion frowned on taking blood transfusions or transfusions with blood-based substances, under any circumstances. However, they both loved me enough to let me make my own decisions regarding health care choices, and so didn't show the disapproval they must have been feeling. Instead, they continued to smile at me tolerantly.

"Your anemia is so serious that if you don't take it, you're liable to die," countered the nurse.

At that moment, feeling as weak as I was, I felt conflicted. Not because of my family's religious qualms, but for entirely different reasons. My hesitancy came from the fact that I had never had a blood transfusion before and hadn't I already had enough infusions! It hadn't helped that the male nurse who had given me the IV of saline had poked my arm in various places before finding the right infusion spot. I hesitated and then agreed to the infusion of plasma since I really did feel that my need for it was urgent. Andy looked at me as if to say, *Go for it!* Robert and Cindy simply smiled, although the look in their eyes showed disapproval.

Quickly, the nurse changed the saline bags for the blood plasma. Before injecting it into me, she had me read the roster of side effects and then sign a paper. I was also made to sign a paper the doctor gave me concerning resuscitating me if I went into shock or cardiac arrest.

"You're young," he told me. "If you were eighty, I might have hesitated having you go through this procedure."

"Thank you for calling me young," I told him. Then as the plasma started going into me, I started talking with my family who had shed their initial reaction to my decision to take the infusion with forbearing love.

"Do you think I could stay with you guys for a while and just relax and heal?" I asked weakly, but hopefully.

"You could stay as long as you wanted too. We'd love to have you," said my brother who was looking at me in a way that was loving as well as worried.

Then I fainted away.

143

When I came too, my brother and sister-in-law were still there and so was Andy. But he had to leave.

"Call me if you need me," reassured my neighbor as he gave me a big hug. "I will look after Pepper for you."

"I'll stay with you, April," said Robert. "This is not a time for a person to be left all alone by themselves, least of all my dear lil'sis."

"But I have to go back home," said Cindy almost apologetically. "Somebody needs to look after Henry." She followed this with a hug full of sisterly affection.

"See you later then, Cindy," I told her. "Love you."

"I love you too, April," she assured me.

Then as Robert took hold of my hand, she turned to Andy who was putting his dark blue baseball cap back on. The copper red design on the front was of Tsagaglal, or "She Who Watches", a regional petroglyph that represents a female chief who, according to legend, was changed into a basalt boulder so that she could watch over her beloved people forever.

"Would you like me to drive you back to your apartment, Andy?" Cindy asked him kindly.

"Thank you, Cindy. I would appreciate that," my friend and neighbor replied. Then he went over to me.

"Be brave, April," he said as he gave me a bear hug that was like food for my anguished soul. "You're going to be fine and you can call me anytime. Pepper will be with me and Skippy the whole time."

"Thank you, Andy," you are a great friend.

"So are you, April, m'dear. And your brother is here to look after you tonight."

"Yes, he is. Thank God for that. Bye for now."

"See you later."

On that note, my sister-in-law and friend left me and my brother. He said a quiet prayer over me as he remained in his seat close by the hospital bed I'd been transferred too. I fell into a fitful sleep. But thankfully, I was given some extra comfort through the whole ordeal. That night, in a dream vision, Billy appeared to me and placed a salmon-shaped bead made of carnelian in my hand.

"You will be all right, April. Tomanowos and I are here to look after you tonight along with your brother," he said as he gently held my hand clasping the red-orange bead. And I did sleep well.

In the morning, my sister-in-law came and got me and my brother, who after his nighttime vigil of looking after me, was glad to get back to his own home and bed. When I was brought to the door of my apartment, Robert showed his love for me even further with a fond invitation.

"Would you like to come over to our place today, just for the afternoon? Then we could talk about you and your dog staying longer," asked my brother.

"No thank you. Maybe some other time," I reluctantly declined.

The truth was, I was feeling a lot better now that the worst of my present ordeal was over. I was no longer in a panic state and I wanted to spend my time with Andy instead. You see, there were some things I felt I needed to talk over with him.

145

When I got back to my apartment complex, I visited with Andy for a while as we watched our dogs sniff around and play together.

"You sure needed that plasma. I believe you probably would've died without it. You were looking positively green yesterday, especially under the eyes," he commented while sipping his coffee.

He offered some to me, but I declined. I hadn't had breakfast yet and it was against my own health rules to take caffeine on an empty stomach.

"Green like the grass and willow leaves beside that funeral home," I commented with a wry smile thinking about how close I had been that afternoon to being a candidate for that place. But Andy had brought me through it all and I felt I was on the mend.

"Andy, there's something I've been meaning to tell you ever since the day you peeled me off the cop car and then the sidewalk," I said cautiously.

"And what would that be, beautiful April?" he asked with a sweet smile.

"I don't want to scare you or sound like I'm coming on too strong, but ever since that day, I've developed feelings of real love for you. I didn't think I could ever feel that way again for any man when Ozzy died," I said looking fondly into his brown eyes, which were gentle, but also carried a lot of strength.

"I'm glad to hear that, April, because I've felt that way about you for years. I was reluctant to tell you so for three reasons. My last marriage was a heart breaker for me. That woman, Cecilia, did things to me you wouldn't believe. Also, I didn't want to seem pushy with you. You've always come across to me as a strong, self-made woman who really didn't have room for a man in her life. Then you needed time for your heart to heal from Ozzy's death. He was a very sweet man, I've heard, and I didn't feel that I could measure up to him," confessed Andy with a touch of longing in his voice that warmed my heart to the core.

"If I was able to earn a lot of money with my books, could I be your girlfriend then, Andy? You can't build a solid relationship without money," I said with sincere hopefulness.

"*Ha ha.* Money's got nothing to do with it as I see it. We can be boyfriend and girlfriend, we can even get married, but first I need a little bit more time to heal from the wounds Cecilia gave me. In the meantime, I love you and, if we both work on it, this love between us will grow. I have every reason to believe that. You see, love isn't something you fall into. It's some-thing you grow between yourself and the person you love," said Andy with a robust grin.

"I agree totally. And I love you so much, Andy, I'm willing to cultivate what's been growing between us like a bed of deli-cious strawberries and give it time," I agreed with new feelings of joy in my heart.

"Mmmm, I love strawberries," said Andy as he rolled his tongue across his lips.

"So do I," I said as I gave him a hug. This time, he gave me a brief kiss on the lips that was sweeter than any strawberry, no matter how ripe.

The next day, we both celebrated midsummer and our newly confessed feelings for each other by eating a strawberry pie I had baked. Andy's love had redeemed the summer and made the torment of July 25th seem very distant.

As it turned out, the ordeal that day was a product of two things. Anemia caused by the chemo since the medicine can reduce a person's red blood cells. But a more critical factor was the hidden blood loss caused by a pre-existing stomach condition. I had learned from the doctor attending me that late afternoon that I had gastritis, a condition bordering on a stomach ulcer. He had discovered that by poking around in my rectum and finding some blood. It didn't help that I had hemorrhoids as well. He had suspected internal bleeding as at least one of the causes of my anemia and was puzzled by its source. He was relieved to find that it did have a tangible root cause, that is, gastritis

To help with my gastritis, he had sent me home with a prescription for Pantoprazole, a powerful acid blocker. I was supposed to take it for a month and as soon as I started it, my stomach began to feel better. Dr. Xiwang would also prescribe iron pills for me.

I realized that my anemia had a third cause – I had inherited it. My father had been anemic. Yeah, guys get it too.

In the days and weeks that followed that terrible day, I recovered and grew stronger. The stomach and iron medications helped. So did prayer times and talks with Andy. Then there was my dog. She also kept my life active and full of hope. I was taking her for longer and longer walks. Now that I was nearing the end of my chemo cycle, with only one more treatment to go, I was regaining my strength. I had stopped going to gym ever since the day I had fainted on the kitchen floor, but I was doing planking on my own floor along with my dog walks. Planking is where a person kneels down on their forearms and toes and remains in that position for a few minutes. Right now I'm doing five minutes, but I'm working my way up to ten.

It was irritating when I got a phone call from MCMC informing me that I had to make an appointment at the request of Nurse Practitioner Poule, for surgery to be done for my gastritis. Politely, I canceled. I already had enough on my hands, medically, to deal with. Besides, my stomach was a lot better. My thought was, *don't fix it if its not broken.* I also believed that the old biddy was trying to meddle in my life this one last time, just to be ornery. It didn't matter, by my next Shaxu appointment, she would replaced with Nurse Jackson.

With my stamina returning, I was feeling better physically. No nausea, constipation, or radical tiredness. Still, the traumas of the potassium scare and being rushed to emergency would remain with me and leave scars. Thank God I had my dog, Andy, and my family to keep me grounded and balanced.

DISASTER TEN

As it was, I was feeling upbeat, inspired, and very positive as I made my way across the Columbia River Bridge to my final chemo treatment. The nurses there were very kind and gentle as they probed me for blood samples and later, had no trouble hooking me up to the infusion machine. Because I had requested it, they set me up so I could use my arm and hand freely. I would be able to write, turn the pages in the book I was reading, and even eat.

My talk with the doctor was so positive that I felt like I was walking on a cloud. My infatuation with him was gone now that I was finding true love in Andy's big arms. Even so, my gratitude toward the good medical man was strong and would remain so. Under Dr. Xiwang's wise guidance I would complete my chemo treatment that day and feel like I'd won a victory.

"I talked with the technician who did your blood tests and made that mistake with your potassium level. That was a serious error she made and I know it caused you terrible emotional trauma. I hope it helps you heal mentally as well as physically to know that I fired her from her job," the doctor informed me with a kind tip of his head, almost as though he was bowing to me.

"Thank you, doctor. That makes me feel like I matter and that I'm not just a rat in a cage," I said beaming.

"I would never want you to feel that way, April. You are a valuable patient to me so I care very much about you. I must add though, please don't blame Nurse Poule for the accident in the lab. Even though she's not your idea of a good nurse, the whole thing was Technician Cheeky Brady's felt and not hers. Still, I know that you don't like working with her, so I've taken her off your case," he continued.

"Thank you, doctor. There's just been a personality clash between me and Nurse Poule. She's a good nurse, actually, she's just not a good one for me," I said with a laugh in my voice.

I was starting to feel more than good, I was beginning to feel like more than a conqueror as described in Romans 8:37. The doctor had more good news for me though.

"Your cancer was aggressive, but it appears to be gone from your breasts and armpits. If it is completely gone from everywhere in your body, we can make sure it stays gone by you taking antibodies and hormone blockers," he said in a way that was hopeful, but left me feeling puzzled.

"May I ask you what antibodies are? Are they something like antibiotics?" I asked, wondering if I'd heard him right.

"Feel free to ask me anything you want to, April. That's what I'm here for. No, antibodies are different from antibiotics. Antibodies are for destroying the pathways that the cancer created in your body. You see, your cancer was HER2 positive. That means it left these pathways and could grow along them if it ever returns," explained Dr. Xiwang with patience and compassion.

"Can I take these in pill form?" I asked hopefully feeling a chill of dread running up and down my spine.

"Of course, I would highly recommend it in your case, April."

"What are the long term affects of taking these kinds of medication?" I asked, dreading his reply.

"Oh, antibodies can be a bit hard on your heart. But someone like you who exercises regularly and watches what they eat isn't likely to have any trouble with that. The other medicine, the hormone blockers, can cause osteoporosis. This too, isn't likely to be a problem if you keep taking calcium supplements and exercising. For your own peace of mind, I can schedule for you to have electrocardiograms and bone density scans regularly," he explained in a way that brought me great relief.

Feeling a bit more encouraged, I showed Dr. Xiwang an article about hormone blockers that was in a publication put out by his own hospital. He read it briefly and then enlightened me further.

"Yes, that article does explain the value of the hormone blockers and I agree with it. Even so, I feel you will need the antibodies for your treatment to be complete. You see, April, what has happened with you is nothing short of a miracle. People in my profession don't like to use the word 'cured' when they describe someone with your condition, but that is the only right word to use here. In your case, it looks so far like the chemo and biologics alone were enough to cure your cancer. Even so, I believe you will need some antibody and hormone blocker pills for this cure to be complete," Dr. Xiwang continued.

"When will I need to start taking these medicines?" I asked, feeling new hope.

"Right after the results of your PET and CT scans come back."

"Thank you, doctor," I said shaking his hand. "When will these tests be scheduled?"

"I will make that appointment for you, April."

"God bless you, doctor."

"And may God bless you, April. I am a strong believer in the power of the Almighty and I believe He did have a hand in your cure."

"I believe so too, doctor."

As I left him, I felt like I was surrounded by guardian angels. My doctor being a God-fearing man had put new faith in my heart and he had all but admitted that my cancer was "cured". I felt then that I had every reason to live and would keep on living a good long time. Aside from possibly needing to have some mop up work done, that is, go on some new medicines, I felt that my cancer was likely all gone, never to return. The dreaded hospice was not in my future. I had gone from a woman who was broken and trying to grasp for a reason to want to keep on living to one starting to see hope and relief over the chemo being nearly completed. This time, I didn't need to put on a fake smile as I joined my brother and Cindy and accepted being hooked up to the infusion.

A few minutes later, the staff brought me and my family a snack plate full of cheese, crackers, and sliced apples. All of us devoured it hungrily. Both of them were kind, agreeable, and attentive to me that day.

But my brother had to leave. He had some purchases in town to make. With a fond clasp of my hand, he told me he'd be back.

"Do you think you could take me to Fred Meyers and Joanne Fabrics?" I asked with a hopeful smile.

"No, it will be too late by the time you're done here."

"Then could you bring me a Hawaiian pizza and a chocolate milkshake from MOD?"

"Yes, we can do that."

Then he and Cindy left. Ensconced in my padded infusion chair, I was content with my writing and book. I was also enjoying talking with a woman named Marilyn who was having her own struggles with cancer. She had taken chemo once for breast cancer. Even so, it had come back. Now she was taking a different brew of medicine. This involved taking antibodies and hormone blockers by infusion.

She was also having trials in different areas of her life. She had been homeless and living under a bridge until then.

"Now I have my own apartment and my own bed," the thin rather pretty woman revealed.

"I'm happy for you," I told her. Then I noticed some picture cards that she had in her lap.

Each one featured a different dominant color. Some were scenes in nature, while others were of art objects. One was of a bronze statue.

"What are those cards about? They sure are pretty," I inquired.

"They are all about color therapy. Did you know that colors can be healing?" she explained as she took the cards out and started leafing through them.

"Yes, I've heard that."

"I was having trouble with back pain because of the effect the hormone treatment was having on my joints. So I laid on this card and it helped strengthen me back there. Most of the pain left," she said as she showed me the bronze card.

"That's interesting," I said.

"What's the color that speaks to you right now?"

"Green."

On that cue, she showed me three cards. One had an emerald green scene with a building in that shade. The next one was all of true green foliage, while the last one was a forest of, you guessed it, forest green. Truthfully, I felt drawn to them all.

"I like the true green one best," I told her, feeling that I had to make some kind of choice.

"That's very good. Green is a healing color," she said as she gave me the card of green leaves and plants.

"Thank you, but are you sure you want to give me this?" I asked.

"I've never been more sure about anything in my life. We are both on the same healing journey," she reassured me.

When I took the card, I did feel better. Maybe there was some hope for me after all. Just then, my brother and sister-in-law were back with the pizza and milkshake. They had already eaten theirs. I thanked them and then started in on my meal. I talked with them about the shopping they had done. Cindy had gotten a new bra, while my brother had purchased some cables in hopes of improving his TV reception. Both of us had the same problem. Because of the weak TV signal in our area, the shows we got would all too often be broken up in pixels or not come in at all. I had a nick-name for this mess. Because the pictures would disintegrate into pixels, I said that this was the work of pixies who infested my TV. I hated this happening nearly every time I tried watching my favorite programs. Perhaps if Robert could solve that problem for his TV, he could solve it for mine. He also suggested I get a better antenna for my TV. I said that I would in the following month.

We also chatted with Marilyn. What she had to say about colors in relation to healing the mind as well as the body was fascinating. When 4:00 rolled around, she left. I thanked her for the green motif card as she walked off. A minute later my IV bag was drained and it was time for me to go too.

But before I left the staff at Shaxu had a big surprise for me. Just as I was about to leave my infusion chair, out came one of the head nurses, Roxie Espèrer, through the door with a small pink frosted cake in her hands. Beside her was my doctor with a grin that was handsomer than ever.

"What's all this about?" I asked with mild amazement.

What was going on here? It wasn't my birthday.

"Just something we like to do for a patient when they complete their round of chemotherapy. This is to celebrate your victory over cancer and how brave you've been the whole time," explained my miracle working and believing doctor.

I was so moved I didn't know what to say. With tears of gratitude in my eyes I ate a piece of the pink cake which had a large pink frosting ribbon in its center and inspiring slogans like, "Hello, new survivor" written all over it in white frosting. My brother and sister-in-law each had a piece too. I would take the rest of it home to snack on another day. This cake provided generously by my helpers at Shaxu made me feel that I was a winner and would stay a winner through whatever remained of my personal cancer fight.

On the way back to Goldendale, I was feeling a bit drowsy but still managed to have a good, uplifting talk with my brother and sister-in-law.

"I talked with your doctor in the hallway and he said he has every reason to believe that your cancer is gone," Robert told me happily.

"Then all of that *eeeeuw* chemo along with my vitamins and prayer really paid off," I replied with a satisfied smile. I was still enjoying the taste of the cake in my mouth. It had actual strawberry flavored frosting.

"Yes, it did, and I'm proud of you. Now all that remains is for you do some preventative care, like taking that medication he suggested," Robert said, his tone growing more serious.

"I need to wait a month before I decided anything. I need to process all this and go into it with a clear head," I said a little defensively.

"That's fine. Dr. Xiwang told me that with everything you've been through, you should rest at least that long before you be-gin any more treatments. That would include treatments with medication," Robert continued, sounding more tender than usual.

At that moment I felt that any victories I had achieved were just the beginnings of opportunities for more. Even in my soul, I knew that I had not gone through the torture of the chemo for nothing.

"I would still prefer pills to infusions. I've had enough of infusions and want a break from them," I insisted knowing what I wanted and what would work for me.

"That's fine, April," your doctor said that you didn't need to go the infusion route again," said my brother meekly.

"Thank God for that," I said happy that I could have some say in my own treatment program.

After I was dropped off at my apartment, I found Andy and we both took our dogs for a walk. When I told him about the party they threw for me at Shaxu, he laughed.

"That was some fun party, April. Kicking cancer is a thing to celebrate," said Andy.

Later that day, he and I had a little celebration of our own. Each of us had a bowl of his good halibut stew followed by several glasses of rich red wine.

I went to sleep that night drifting into joyful slumber with Pepper cuddling close by my side. To add to my nocturnal pleasure, Billy and his puppets came to me with a very special song and dance routine. When I met him in the vacant lot, he put on a puppet show featuring two puppets that he had made with the forms and features of my brother and sister-in-law. They did a sock hop dance and sang me a song about whether my cancer came back or not, it didn't matter. Even how much more time I had left on this sometimes dreary, sometimes sweet, Earth wasn't important either. What was important was my using however much time I still had left to show love to my brother, sister-in-law, dog, and now, Andy. Equally important though were my books. I was to market them to the best of my knowledge and ability, but not tax myself too badly about doing that part, that is, the sales angle. I had fulfilled a large part of my destiny by simply writing them.

"Each book contains a wealth of inspiration and wisdom for whoever reads it," explained Billy as he put the puppets away. Up above us, the moon was shining in a way that brought me great comfort.

"Whether you should take further treatments for preventing cancer returns, The Great Spirit has not put it on me to tell you. Nor can I tell you what forms they should take. Actually, it doesn't matter and trust me, I know this one bit of truth. No matter what you do or don't do, you are not going to die any-time soon," as Billy related this, he brought out some smudge sticks and lit them. Then he began softly pounding on a deer skin covered drum.

The image of the guardian on the wall near us beamed at me as the smoke grew thicker and the drum became steadier and louder. Then I was gone and in my own bed. I finished my sleep feeling that I had forgiven everyone and was at peace with everyone.

The next morning I awoke feeling happy and vigorous – I really was not going to die anytime soon. Pepper was licking me in the face with love and gusto. It was going to be a great day!

DISASTER ELEVEN

The rest of August blazed on for me and I felt hot and happy. I went for another PET scan which was coupled with a CT scan. This happened on August 21st at ten o'clock. It made me feel better that it was done in The Dalles rather in Portland at the Epic Imaging building which was still in the process of being built. I was to be taken to my appointment by faithful Cindy who was also relieved that we didn't need to go all of the way to "Ripcity", as Portland is sometimes called. I endured the routine of following the same instructions I had been forced to obey months earlier when I was given the PET/MRI scans. I ate no breakfast, abstained from sugar the day before, and drank a full eight glasses of water. Before leaving, I took Pepper for her early morning walk and then left her with Andy.

The session with the PET machine, which would handle both scans, was all to happen in the trailer of a semi truck. This trailer was only slightly larger than big truck trailers usually were. I reported, with my sister-in-law beside me, to the clinic this trailer was parked beside. I signed a bunch of papers and then Cindy waited in the clinic lobby while a nurse led me to the big truck trailer. I rode a ramp which pulled me up to the trailer's main entrance. There was a roar of mighty hydraulics as the door opened and I was led into a compact chamber of lights and electronic machinery. I felt a little overwhelmed as the technician invited me to sit down and prepare to have my blood taken. Feeling numb, I complied.

He did run into some unexpected problems, however. The serious-faced, thin young man tried all over my hands and arms to find a vein that would cooperate with his efforts to take a blood sample.

"I have always succeeded in finding a spot. I have never failed," he said with increasing frustration. I said nothing, but was getting very tired of being a pin cushion.

"Well, this might be the time I'm humbled," the technician concluded. "There probably had to come a day when I would finally find somebody with veins I can't work."

I thought his remarks, though meant to be humorous, were a little on the insensitive side. He was just about ready to call for back-up from a person who was skilled in handling truly difficult veins, when suddenly, he found one in the back of my hand that would hold up for him.

"Your chemo treatment sure didn't do your veins any good. They're tougher than usual," he explained as the blood poured from the wire into the test tube. "But I've seen it before with other oncology patients."

So why did he make it sound like I was the first one with challenging veins? I wondered to myself.

Obviously, the man was someone who liked to indulge in useless talk.

I was feeling a bit ill-used by the time the technician was through taking my blood and had given it to another technician to be analyzed for high blood sugar. In a half hour the results came back. Sure enough, I wasn't diabetic. But I could have told them as much.

It was required procedure that I be tested for diabetes, since the tracer fluid I would be given to facilitate the scans was a radioactive fluid with a heavy glucose base. I worried more about it being radioactive, but said nothing. With all of the radioactive fluids I had already been given, however, it wouldn't have surprised me if I glowed in the dark and triggered beeps from a Geiger counter.

On considering the glucose factor of the tracer fluid, I thought not of myself but of my new boyfriend, Andy, who has a hard case of type 2 diabetes. I wondered how someone like him would be prepared for a scan like what I was going to be put through. Surely, they couldn't give him the same tracer.

Soon after that diagnosis was done, I was given the tracer infusions and then told to rest. I was even supposed to keep my eyes closed since any muscle activity, no matter how slight, was likely to affect the result of the scans. I was feeling drowsy anyway, so I just laid back and rested for another half hour. The lights of the trailer were dimmed so that it would be easier for me to do so. I didn't sleep, but put my mind to daydreaming about being somewhere else, like on another planet where there was no cancer and I was in the arms of my darling Andy who thought the world of me.

I wasn't long into this reverie before the thin, rather plain technician drew back the drapes of my cubicle and told me that it was time for me to be loaded into the PET machine. With an Aspartame smile, I slipped on the white hospital gown I was given and let myself be loaded unto the gently moving, cushioned conveyor belt that would bring me into the mouth of the glittering, foreboding device. First, I would be given the CT (Computed Tomography) scan. This first test is like an X-ray only much more detailed. It is able to show what is going on, including where small cells of cancer might be lurking, in every region of the body all at once. I was told to put my arms up over my head as I rode in for first this scan and then the other. I kept my eyes closed the whole time, dreading what I might see. Later, I was told that I hadn't needed to do that. Still, keeping my eyes closed made me feel more secure.

"Thank you for being such a cooperative patient. You are the best one I've seen in a long while," remarked the bony young technician.

In reply, I smiled sweetly and thanked him for calling me that, while inside I sneered at him for making snide remarks about my "tough veins". After removing myself from the padded conveyor belt, I was directed back to my former cubicle where I removed the gown and put my clothes back on. The nurse then led me to the reception lobby where I met up with Cindy.

"Don't worry, April. I believe there's every chance both scans will show that you are clean of the cancer," she said while giving me a strong hug.

"I agree, Cindy," I said in a hopeful voice. "No cancer could have survived what all I've been put through, especially with that nurse and her arm boards."

Both of us laughed at that. Then we walked over to the receptionist whom I asked to confirm for me when I would get the results from my tests.

"We find the results of tests like those within twenty-four hours," said the receptionist with a sweetness I found tiring. Still, her reply satisfied me.

Both me and Cindy were hungry, especially me since it was nearing noon and I hadn't eaten a bite. So we drove over to MOD, home of the world's best pizza and most eccentric pizza servers. I ordered a small pizza for both of us along with milk shakes. While doing so, I noticed that the girl who served our meal was wearing a T-shirt that had a goofy smiley face along with the words "Keep MOD Weird".

"I really like your shirt. It sends chills of delight up and down my spine," I remarked as I dove hungrily into my ham, cheese, and pineapple pizza.

"Glad you like it. It makes me happy to wear it and I try to wear it everywhere. Good advertisement for this place," she replied.

"That's so clever!" I said with enthusiasm.

"Hey, we have 'em for sale here. Would you like one too?" she asked as Cindy gave me a wink as if to say *go ahead and get one.*

"I would. Wearing it would cheer me up. You see, I've been doing cancer treatment and I'm better now. But the whole experience has been eeeeuw!" as I said this, I bravely peeled off my wig, exposing my bare-naked head.

Nobody there looked at me strange or acted scared. In fact the server girl looked at me in a way that was very sympathetic.

"You look beautiful without your wig. Why don't you just keep it off. This is the one place where everyone can be who they are and look like themselves without people jumping on them," reassured the daring young woman.

"Yes, April, you look great with or without your wig," joined in Cindy who was nibbling away at her own pizza slice.

So, with the encouragement of both these fine ladies, I finished off my pizza and blueberry milkshake bareheaded and unashamed. I had to admit that I really didn't look half bad and caught a few of the men present casting admiring looks my way. When I was done with my meal and Cindy was done with hers, I did put my wig back on, however. I had a few places to go and wasn't quite brave enough to face the world hairlessly.

Cindy and I both did some shopping at Fred Meyers. Then I bought some sewing supplies at Joann Fabrics. I planned to make some dolls to sell along with my books.

In the days and weeks following my PET/CT scan, I went along with my life and waited for news of the results. I wanted to believe that all that chemo I had endured had made me cancer-free. Even so, it was hard for me not to be apprehensive. Cindy told me not to borrow trouble about it and Katie told me about the same thing, as did Andy. Billy in my dreams gave me similar assurances.

Meanwhile, as August drew to a crisp close and the leaves of local trees were starting to turn bright yellow, I went to the Klickitat County Fair with Robert. To my surprise and delight, he came and got me in the little yellow car that he had made himself. This vehicle, he had modeled roughly along the lines of a Model T-Ford, although it had an up-to-date engine and other modern internal workings. I always love riding in it.

Throughout my time at the fair, I enjoyed watching a rodeo, looking over the exhibits, and just walking around in the dry fields near the grounds. During one of these walks, I saw Mount St. Helens, the decapitated mountain, off in the distance and took a photo of it. My brother was there to help man the Search And Rescue booth, since he is an active member of that vital organization. I sat with him there and talked with him and some of people who also served in that group. I learned while listening to him talk with them that Goldendale had recently been invaded by a mountain lion. This big cat had made quite a dire nuisance of himself by going into someone's yard and eating a raccoon. Seemingly, a wild "straight gut", he had then devoured a fawn and doe who had also wandered into the yard. He was about ready to start in on the family terrier when animal control confronted him and shot him. Later on, these officers found a chilling sight in the cougar's deep woods den. Littering it were the skeletons of many pet dogs and cats he had gorged on. Had animal control not offed him, his menu would have likely began to include small children as well.

After listening to that thrilling account of the cougar who invaded Goldendale, I left to look over the animal exhibits. I saw cattle in one barn, while the horses were in another. The rabbits and chickens also had their special building. While I was looking over the rabbits, two very sweet little girls let me hold one. Afterward, I went to look at the goats and sheep. Seeing the goats brought me special memories since I had helped raise ones like them when I was a kid in Canada. I went to look over the horses and was pleased by how well-groomed they looked. They were not only clean, but also well-brushed. They also were in stalls that were the best decorated of all the animal stalls. Many were adorned with stars made of barbed wire. I thought it would be fun to have a decoration like that, maybe for my door. Of all the animals, however, the most amusing were the pigs. It made me laugh the way they stuck their snouts through the grills of their stalls and snorted. Indeed, their snorts alone made me laugh.

"I think the pig is the most comical creature God ever created," I confessed to Andy the next day.

"Yes, they are, but you'd be surprised at how smart they are and how good they are at using their noses for digging. My father had a pig just for going out and finding truffles. When he found them, that pig would really go at it and dig them up. It was really fun to watch," said Andy as his brown eyes shown with the tenderness that comes with recalling happy memories.

During my time at the fair, there was another animal I made acquaintance with and one that outdid them all, hands down. Some people brought a "dinosaur" in a trailer to the fairgrounds and one man led "her" around, letting people pet her and eat a treat, like a chicken tender, now and then. Several people had their pictures taken with her and I took a few photos of the lumbering reptile. Her name was Susie and though she was a tyrannosaurus, she was every inch gentle and domesticated.

That day I heard several people remark about the guy that was supposedly in "that dinosaur suit". He must be very uncomfortable, they insisted. Fit to roast, in fact. But I knew better. I had seen documentaries about robot dinosaurs in places like OMSI, The Oregon Museum of Science and Industry, which is sort of like a small, science-oriented Disneyland. From watching TV shows featuring similar automatons, I knew that Susie was a robot rather than some dude in a dinosaur suit. I could tell by the way she was controlled by her handler's remote control device. Still, I played along. It was fun for me to pretend the creature was real. A lot of other people thought it was fun too.

"You better not get too close behind that thing. It's liable to make some big piles," said a man of about fifty to his grandchildren who were only inches from the dinosaur's big scaly rump.

To my disappointment, however, I never saw her leave any poop piles behind. An impish part of me wishes that she had. It would have added to the realism.

Another feature at the fair that really intrigued me was a rock that had been struck by lightning. It was on display at the booth manned by the town's local PUD, Public Utility District, department. Somehow this stone and the realistic dinosaur both reminded me of Tomanowos and its own ancient origins.

ℛ ℛ ℛ

In the days that followed my romp at the fair, I waited for news about my PET/CT scans. Twice I phoned MCMC about it, then I phoned Shaxu. The reply was always the same.

"It's the duty of your doctor to give you this data, not us. We gave the results of your scans to your doctor, so he should be calling you about that," I was told by the receptionist at Shaxu.

Then four days after my last phone call to Shaxu, I got the news that I had been eager to receive ever since my PET/CT scans were given.

"Your scans show that your cancer is gone completely," said Dr. Xiwang.

"Even the spot on my liver?" I asked, delighted but still hardly believing my ears.

"Yes, even the spot on your liver," he answered with a note of cheer in his voice.

"Okay. Thank you for the good news. Now where should I go from here with this cancer treatment program?" I asked sweetly, ready for just about anything.

"You can come back here for check-ups every three months and I'll just prescribe the hormone blocker and antibody medications for you. That's about all the treatment you'll need from on," Dr. Xiwang advised kindly.

At that, I thanked him again and then we said our good byes. I thought for a moment of making an appointment with him, but

168

then I decided to wait. That night I had a dream that determined my next course of action. In it, I met with Billy who put on a puppet show featuring a dancing doll dressed like a lady doctor.

"April, Dr. Xiwang has been a good doctor for you, but it is time for you to move on," Billy explained as he put the puppet aside and the smoke of smudge sticks curled up to the black, star-studded sky. I breathed deep the pungent aroma.

"Where am I to move on to?" I asked my spiritual guide who was looking both wise and handsome with his long braids and beaded buckskin.

"Knight Cancer Institute. That is where your future healing will spring from. There is a woman doctor who works there who will be of most benefit to you," explained Billy.

A moment later, he was gone and I was left standing there staring at a stack of empty wooden crates. My mind was full of a crate box load of questions. Where was Knight Cancer Institute and who was this lady doctor who was to supplant Dr. Xiwang?

The next day, I looked up the address and phone number of Knight Cancer Institute on the internet and also found the name of a doctor there who seemed to be the one I was looking for. Her name was Dr. Alice Jia Li and she was an oncologist who specialized in breast cancer cases. I contacted Tamara and Kevin Finster who happened to be two very supportive friends from the Seventh-Day Adventist Church. I heard them mention the Knight Cancer Institute once, so I approached them both with questions about this hospital. They recommended it highly, especially since she, Tamara, had gone to it to have some precancerous skin lesions removed.

169

When I asked the Finsters if they would take me to Knight Cancer Institute, which happened to be in Portland, they both agreed they would. They just had to know the time and day of my appointment. It turned out that my initial visit with Dr. Jia Li would be on September 3rd. This was a little awkward because that would be my bill-paying and errand day. My Social Security and SSI monies always come on the 3rd of each month, unless the 3rd happens to be a Saturday or a Sunday. Then my checks arrive at my bank on the Friday preceding. That parti- cular 3rd day turned out to be a Tuesday. I coped with this dilem- ma by planning to pay my bills a day in advance and by making plans to do my major shopping in Portland following my appoint- ment. I am getting better at planning activities. In fact, I am bet- ter at figuring out schedules now than when I was younger.

When the third day of September came around, I went with my friends to Knight Cancer Institute. I was apprehensive, in fact I was nervous out of my mind, but this new lady doctor was very nice and did everything she could to make me feel more at ease. It heartened me that she was Asian, in fact she was a young Asian, which was all to the good. After talking with her, she decided to put me on some pills that would prevent my body from making estrogen, so there would be less of that hormone to bind with any lingering cancer cells and make more tumors. Really, I had a choice of two different pills. One was the hormone blocker already described. The other one prevented the estrogen in my body from binding with whatever cancer cells might still be lurking in my body. The first type, called anastrozole, was hard on the bones causing possible osteoporosis and joint pain. The latter, tamoxifen, had a lot more frightening side effects. These included the chance of strokes, blood clots, and heart attacks. Added to this grim list were other less potentially fatal but still seriously bothersome side effects like mood swings and weight gain. I decided to opt for the anastrozole, while continuing to take calcium and avoid falls as much as possible. I would take a bone scan once a year too, though not any oftener. But no matter what, I would never take those medicines for building bone density. I heard of taking them resulting in some really horrific side effects, like causing the jaw bone to deteriorate.

Of course, the intravenous hormone blockers and antibodies would be even harder on the heart than the tamoxifen. So much so, that I would need to have another heart monitor check-up before I even went on them. That was something I wanted to avoid if at all possible. Dr. Jia Li told me that antibodies were advisable since I had a cancer that was HR2 positive, that is, related to a hormone that had created what was known as "cancer pathways". The cancer itself was gone, but there still were these pathways it could follow if it ever came back. These pathways could lead, she explained to places like my brain or bowels.

But she respected my decision to avoid or at least delay taking the intravenous antibodies. I felt that I had suffered enough with intravenous treatments, because of the chemo and because of having to take the blood transfusion.

"You have been through some really rough times and you just need to rest. I will keep track of you to make sure your cancer doesn't come back. If it does, then you will probably have to take the antibodies, but you won't need to take either them or the hormone blocker intravenously," she said cautiously, but with great sympathy.

"That sounds like the best bet to me," I told her. "Thank you."

"You're very welcome and very brave too. In the meantime, I will want to see you in a month from now and I will prescribe anastrozole for you now," Dr. Jia Li added with a kind under-standing smile.

"Sounds like the best plan yet. I've really been having panic

171

attacks just thinking about going on more infusions," I added, feeling very relieved.
"Well, you won't need too. You can take everything in pill form including the antibodies. But don't even think about that now. Just rest," said Dr. Jia Li as my friends looked on and smiled with approval.

"I will," I said as I grasped the lady's hand with tender thanks.

After my appointment, my friends and I went to three different grocery stores that sold produce very cheap. I'll have to confess that these stores had some really good bargains, if you knew what you were looking for. There was also a lot of cruddy molded stuff too, however. After picking up some fairly good fruits and vegetables, my friends and I went to a second hand store. In there, I found some good cloth for making doll clothes and a book about the famous Spanish painter, Pablo Ruiz Picasso. This tome was chock full of pictures of his paintings, from his more famous abstracts to his lesser known sketches. A real treat for the eye!

I ate a sandwich that Tamara had made for me. It was a veggie burger on whole wheat with homemade ketchup and home grown lettuce, and tomatoes. I found it to be actually quite yummy, even though I am not a strict vegan or even a vegetarian. Tamara had made similar sandwiches for herself and her husband, while I had shared some banana cake I had made with them. They both told me it was delicious.

As I munched on my sandwich, Kevin drove to a health store, called Mother Earth's Bounty, which stood in the countryside on the far outskirts of Portland. While there, I was introduced to the lady who owned the shop, since she was a close friend of Tamara and Kevin. I bought some echinacea capsules and a bag full of salty organic treats which are known as wild rice sticks. Just before we left, we sat with this lady, whose name was Jill Haines, out on a picnic table and did some really involved praying.

After returning to Goldendale, my friends dropped me off at my apartment. Before putting my produce away, I went to check on Pepper. There she was lying fast asleep in her little fur-lined basket. I watched her snooze for a few moments, then she slowly came awake, stretching her furry little legs and with her long pink tongue curling out in an arc. I told her "hello" and then picked her up, preparing to take her for a walk. It was not quite dark yet and the sun was just starting to set in a glow of orange fading rays and clouds of soft creamy white. I put her on her leash and carried her lovingly down the stairs. When we were outside the apartment complex door, I put her down and enjoyed the sound of crickets that greeted us all around along with the cooing of a dove. Pepper was alright, so all was right with the world as a whole.

REDEMPTION

The next morning I got up feeling more enthused then usual and ready to face the tasks of the day with alacrity. I fed Pepper and then took her out for her morning run. It was very early morning and the sun was just coming up in a burst of salmon pink. The leaves were only beginning to turn color. Some were red, some were yellow, while some were the deepest purple. My dog and I had a good refreshing walk. Afterwards, I brought her back to my apartment and then took off for my morning run which involved the distance from my apartment complex's sidewalk to the telephone pole near the town's neon cross-topped grain elevators. The original builder of the towers had placed the crucifix there not only as an emblem of faith, but as a way of keeping planes from slamming into them.

After returning from my run, I went back to bed and slept for an hour. After that short time of refreshment, I did a half-hour of exercises. By that time, I was very hungry and ready for breakfast. That was when my day took a turn for the worse. As I was preparing to make some hot oatmeal for myself, I accidentally dropped a spoon on the kitchen floor.

"Cut it out, April, or I'll slap you good! You damn idiot!" came the irate voice of Johnny Dinks in apartment ten directly below me.

Many of us at the Golden Sands had been having continuous problems with this tenant who was more than a little on the wacky side and to make it worse had a very foul temper and a mouth to match. It was 9:00 in the morning and according to the apartment's rules, I was permitted to make ordinary kitchen noises from that time until 9:00 at night.

I felt frightened and went into tears. Not knowing what else to do, I knocked on the door of my neighbor, Selma, who lived in the apartment right across from me.

"What's up?" she asked groggily as she stuck her pretty brunette head through the crack of her door.

All the while she struggled to keep her cat "Penny" from getting out. Penny was still a kitten and when she saw me was as curious as she was lively.

"It's that mean guy directly below me," I protested tearfully. "He screamed threats and insults at me. Actually called me a 'damn idiot'. I would like to go knock on his door and tell him not to come down on me so hard and that I'm not a damn idiot. Would you come with me, Selma?"

"I would call management and complain about him. They are the ones who are in a position to help you with him. I can't help you, April, but I'm sorry he did that to you," Selma said with kind patience.

"Alright, I'll phone the land lord and land lady and tell them about that creep," I said, very disappointed that she wasn't going to go with me and back me up while I confronted the guy.

Still, I knew my neighbor, who really thought a lot of me, was right. She and I going to knock on his door and telling him that he shouldn't have called me what he did would have just antagonized the mean old cuss further. It had worked that way when Mr. Dinks had aroused my boyfriend Andy's ire by blaring his TV loud enough to wake up the whole apartment complex at three in the morning earlier in January. The two men had gotten into a knock down drag out battle. Unfortunately, Andy had gotten the blame for the whole scuffle since he had punched the skinny older fellow hard enough to leave bad bruises.

"It just wasn't fair, Andy dear. Johnny started the fight by having his TV on loud and then aiming a punch at you," I had told Andy over coffee at his place shortly after the incident happened.

"I know, ma'dear, but he got beat up the worst, so I'm the one being pinned for the blame. It's not fair, but I wasn't thinking straight that night. If I hadn't been so groggy tired myself, I would have called our landlord and made a complaint," said Andy with sad regret.

"Don't be so hard on yourself, Andy sweetie. Nobody thinks 100% percent straight that early in the morning," I said in a tone that was meant to be reassuring and supportive.

"That's true, April. Very true," Andy agreed with a fond smile as he took a bite of some peach cobbler I had made and brought to go with our coffee that morning.

Luckily, because Mr. Dinks had started the spat and was so universally disliked by most of us at the Golden Sands, Andy was to receive no legal penalties for blacking both his eyes. Even so, my sweetheart's hard lesson had taught me the value of keeping calm and referring my problems to the right people in charge.

"Yes, I will call Sally and Kenny. Sorry for waking you up," I told Selma as I gave Penny a few gentle strokes on her furry little head.

"Don't think twice about it. I was already up and moving around," said my neighbor with a tolerant smile.

She was used to my getting upset and needing her support at odd hours of the day. She also knew that I couldn't help it and, furthermore, that I was often emotional support for her when she needed it the most. As Selma grabbed up her cat, I thanked her and went back to my own apartment to phone Sally Banister who was the one who was usually there in the office that ran both the Golden Sands and Golden Arms. Her husband, Kenny, was almost never in the office. As a rule, he was out and about doing the maintenance chores that always come with running an apartment. Always there were windows that needed recaulking and sinks and toilets that needed plumbing work.

But Sally wasn't in that morning. So I left her a message. Truly disappointed and dismayed I went to find Pepper who was laying in her little fur lined basket in my bedroom. I gathered her up in my arms and just cried. How I hated to be still living in that apartment complex where I was at the mercy of landlords and had to put up with ugly customers like Johnny Dinks. After I had cried my eyes out for a while, I heard my cell phone ring. When I opened it and answered it, I heard dear Andy's sweet, comforting voice on the other end.

"Hi, April love, how's your morning been so far?" he asked, sounding as bright and cheerful as the autumn sun that was bathing my balcony in gleaming light.

"Pepper and I are both doing okay, but Mr. Dinks sort of spoiled it for me this morning," I replied though I really was feeling much better now that I was talking with Andy. He had a way of cheering me up in even the most doleful times.

"Oh him. What did that fart do this time?" asked my darling man.

"Would you believe that he actually screamed at me for dropping a spoon on my kitchen floor? Called me a 'damn idiot'."

"That was just wrong! Have you reported him to Sally yet?"

"I phoned her at the office and left a message about him."

"You did all you could, April. I know her and Kenny will read your message when they return to their office and do something about dinky old Dinks. He might even lose his apartment this time."

"I sincerely hope he does, Andy. That man has been a pain in the ass for way too long."

"Yes, he has. So, why don't we leave it at that and you bring Pepper down to my place. We can have coffee and I have something to tell you that's so wonderful you'll forget all about Dinks."

"Good, we'll be down in a minute."

"See you in a few."

I closed the lid on my phone and got ready for the coffee klatch. I was already wearing my black turban, so I put on a pair of silver and turquoise earrings. I also put on false eyelashes and plenty of eye make-up to overcome the lingering effects of my chemo treatment which had thinned out my eyebrows and eyelashes. My hair was starting to grow back, but it was still as stubbly as a dry grass field in the Simcoe Mountains. I put on rose pink lipstick and nail polish and grabbed some oatmeal cookies I had baked the day before. I hooked up Pepper to her leash and with all of these things in hand, started down the stairs to my boyfriend's number 14 apartment. I found his door ajar and came in. I put my dog on the wooden floor and unhooked her. There, coming to greet us with a wagging tail and a round of barking was little Skippy. Close beside him was Andy, all smiles.

"Oh, oh, here come the burglers," he said teasingly as he opened his strong arms to give me a good hug.

"*Ha ha.* No, just the neighborhood pick-pockets and wallet snatchers. So, you better hide your wallet," I said returning his tease as I laid the cookies on his crowded kitchen built-ins. Then I flung myself into his arms.

"I really needed that April hug. I miss it on the days when you don't come over," said Andy as he embellished his hug by snuggling his bearded face at my neck.

"And I love my Andy hugs and miss 'em too," I said as I enjoyed the sweet man's closeness.

Just then, Skippy began barking, craving attention.

"Jealous butthead," said Andy in a teasing tone.

"Oh, he just naturally wants some affection too," I remarked with a laugh as I bent over to pet the eager little dog.

After giving him and Pepper some pats on the head, I followed Andy into his living room where I sat down on his elk hide-covered sofa. We sat down beside each other and he gave me a glass mug full of steaming black coffee. He had his beverage in a chinaware mug with a most clever saying on it and pictures of black bears rummaging through a forest. "Don't feed the fears" read the caption.

"You'll never guess who I dreamed about last night?" said Andy as he leaned close to me as though he were about to confide a secret.

"Who? I can't imagine," I replied as I sipped my coffee, my curiosity already starting to build. Across from us, our two dogs were sharing a spot on a blanket in the late-morning sun.

"Billy Brave Salmon," said Andy as he took a sip of his own hot coffee. He liked his dark and plain too.

"Really? That's a switch. Usually, he only comes to me, like he did last night. That's why I woke up this morning feeling better. That is until the Dink raised his ugly voice."

"Never mind him. How did your dream go?"

"It began with Billy standing and confronting some horrible round reddish thing, obviously my tumor. And it was huge, Andy. Nearly as tall as he was. 'Surrender or be destroyed!' it ordered in a voice that had a sucking quality, like a voice coming from a grave. But Billy wasn't the least bit afraid of the noxious thing. 'This is the voice of April's spiritual guide and healer. Negative on surrender. We will not stand down,' he replied to it. 'Who is this? Identify yourself!' demanded the tumor menacingly. 'Who am I? I am Billy Brave Salmon, son of Joe Great Elk,' said my dream hero calmly, but forcefully. 'I am the right hand of vengeance and the callused foot that is going to kick your sorry ass out of April and back to Hell where you belong. I am healing incarnate and the last living thing that you'll ever see. The Great Spirit sent me!' After saying that last bit, Billy kicked that tumor so hard that it went to a place too far away for me to see. Then he turned to me. 'Rest assured, April,' he told me. 'Your cancer is gone, never to return. Believe on that.' An instant later, he was gone into the mists of the night, but he left me with the firm belief that the cancer is completely gone from my body and will never return."

After relating my dream, I turned to Andy. His gentle, but strong eyes were brimming with tears.

"Wow, April. That was powerful. Overwhelming really. I believe that it's true. That the cancer is gone and now all you have to do is finish healing from the chemo treatment. As I said before, chemo is tough medicine," said Andy as he looked at me thoughtfully.

"It was eeeuw, but I'm glad I went through it. It got rid of my tumors," I said, feeling deeply moved myself.

"It saved your life, April," added Andy as he took a big drink from his coffee.

"Indeed, it did. Now, how did your dream with Billy go?" I insisted.

"My dream went like this. He came to me after I drifted off last night. I knew it was him from the way you had described him to me before, with the long braids and necklace with the salmon- shaped pendant. 'Andy,' he said to me. 'I can take you and April to a truly different world where things go happily most of the time and where you can escape the awfulness of this one for awhile.' 'What is it, like on another planet?' I wanted to know. 'No,' he laughed. 'More like another realm or plane of existence. Other planets, no matter how distant, are still just part and parcel of this level of life with all of its horrid limitations and draw- backs. This is life without so many negative factors.' 'Will it look anything like this world or will it look completely alien?' I continued, feeling more and more fascinated by this 'other realm' Billy was describing. 'It will look exactly like this Mother Earth, it will just be closer to perfection,' Billy said. 'Very well, how can April and I get to it?' I ventured to ask. 'Go with her to the shore of the Columbia River where you will see a boat called 'Queen of The Klickitat'. On board is a man who will help you on this journey. His name is Captain Tomas Gresham. He's already been told about you two,' after saying that, Billy vanished and I woke up in my bed. What do you think, April?"

"I think, my friend, that we should finish our coffee, grab the dogs, and drive to that spot where most of the boats dock at the

Columbia River's piers," I told him since I was always ripe for any adventure, no matter how far fetched it might sound.

"I'm good to go, April sweetie. So lets get in my truck," said Andy as he swallowed the last of his coffee.

Since that day in July when he gallantly scooped me up off the police car and then the sidewalk, he had gotten his driving license back. He now had a bright blue Dodge Ram truck.

In a moment, I drained my own cup, put it in the sink, and picked up my dog with Skippy tagging along right beside me. Andy led us to where his worse for wear, but very drivable vehicle stood in the apartment complex parking lot.

"Here we go!" he exclaimed as he got it started and we were on our way.

We rode out of town past trees that were becoming more bare and lines of local houses. Before long, we had made it to the boulder littered banks of the mighty, rolling river. Glancing at the pine and grass adorned islands that studded it and the gray basalt cliffs that towered over it, we found our way to the docking area. Sure enough, there at one of the piers was a large yellow motorboat with the name "Queen of the Klickitat" gracing its side in royal blue letters. And we saw a man, of some height and almost regal baring standing beside it on the dock. He waved and Andy and I waved back.

"That must be Captain Gresham," I said leaning over to my companion.

"It is him. Now I'll park this truck and we can all say "hi" to him," Said Andy as he brought his vehicle over to the parking area and eased it into a spot.

With the dogs following right beside us, we came over to the boat and greeted its captain. I noticed that he had wavy brown hair, intense blue eyes, and a trim mustache.

"Welcome aboard for a great adventure, Andy and April!" he said with jovial humor as he shook our hands.

"We're ready, Captain," said Andy as he climbed on board and then helped pull me on deck. Afterwards, he took both dogs under his arms and brought them on board.

"I love riding on the Columbia and it's a perfect day today, captain. The waves are high but not too rough and the sky above is practically cloudless," I remarked as I turned to look at the river's rushing waters and then gave our host a smile.

He smiled back and then invited us to take seats in the boat.

"I will be manning the controls of the boat, but it's going to be a leisurely trip with plenty of time for us to talk and share stories," The captain explained and I noticed that our passenger seats would be close enough to the steering section for him and us to hear each other well and engage in a lot of lively talk.

Andy and I took our places with a dog on our laps while Captain Gresham unhooked the mooring and sat down in the driver's seat.

"Here we go!" he exclaimed as he turned the key in the ignition and started up the engine. With a mighty roar we were off.

For a while, The Klickitat Queen rode the waves like a dashing dolphin. I watched with breathless excitement as we sped from the shore and past the basalt walls that surrounded us. We went under the bridge and past a grouping of some small islands which appeared to be only inhabited by bushes and trees. When the boat neared a grassy peninsula, the captain slowed the craft down and put it in idle. Turning to us with his hands on his knees he began talking.

"This is not my first time on this huge river. I have rode its waves many times during my career as a barge captain. But I am not from around here. I was born and raised in Ellworth, Maine. My father was a sailor who served in the Korean War and being his only son, I have always been drawn to the water. At the age of three, I made paper boats and floated whole fleets of them off the coast of my hometown. When my father retired from the Navy, I would go with him on crabbing and fishing jaunts in his big fishing boat. The Atlantic Ocean was my life and it never failed to fascinate me.

I was also greatly fascinated by maps as a young boy. I would look for hours at the maps of every continent and became lost in daydreams of going to all those places. I contemplated what each had in store that was unique regarding mountains, cities, and rivers. When a country or city aroused my special interest I would put my finger on it and say, 'I plan to hop on a boat and go here when I'm all grown up.' I recall that Antarctica was one of those places. Even so, I've never been there and I suppose I never will. So many people have been there before and written their accounts of Antarctic adventures that I've simply lost interest in that ice-bound continent. Other spots of interest were scattered in and around South America and in both hemispheres and all latitudes. I have visited some of them. Bimini was a locale of special intrigue for me what with all of its subterranean and undersea structures and artifacts – many of which are reputed to have once been part of the myth- ological continent of Atlantis. But I have already said enough about that. I would rather talk about the locale that peeked my interest and travel lust the most from the very beginning. The jungles of Laos.

On hearing mention of that nation in Southeast Asia, the man had my full attention. That part of the Orient is often the focus of novels I've written through the years.

"Please continue," I begged as Pepper wiggled in my lap.

I put her down and gave her a piece of beef jerky I had in my pocket. Skippy looked on hungrily as my Schnauzer gobbled it up. Unfortunately, I only had enough for one dog. Andy, however, came to his dog's rescue with a bacon flavored dog biscuit.

"Never fear, buddy boy," Skippy's loving pet poppa reassured him as he quickly ate the treat. "You aren't going to be left out."

Captain Gresham laughed at the doggie interlude and continued.

"Although by the time I got to it, that place of lush jungle and stilted village huts had been well-traveled and, even more unfortunately, well-fought over, it still boasted places of wonder and mystery. One of these was the mighty Mekong River. Like a great blue snake it coils up the entire length of the country with tributaries, like snake hatchlings, wriggling out in every direction. Like the Nile is for Egypt, the Mekong is for Laos and the other so-called Indochinese nations. It is mother and nourisher. But it can also be a destroyer which pulls the unwary down into weed-choked depths. Before I even forded it, I both feared and adored the great river and was determined to make it mine.

I made inquiries and learned of an American-based trading company working on that river. Morry's Exotics, it was called. It wasn't doing well and it dawned on me what I could do to help that business grow. They would need the right kind of boats and plenty of them. With what resources I had, I made plans to be that foundering company's boat supplier. At that point, I contacted the head of Morry's Exotics. In reply, he told me that if I could produce the ships, he would become partners with me. I agreed, and got to work building my fleet. First, I sold the off coast fishing business I had inherited from my father and, along with a sizable sum of money he willed to me following his death from a heart attack, used it all to buy a couple of large freighters.

The man in charge of Morry's Exotics was impressed and we signed a contract in his central office in New York City. Of course, more ships would be purchased as our business grew. I would stay in Laos and be in charge of these ships.

After I first arrived in that Asian backwater, something very fortuitous happened that sped my plans forward like the motor of a speed boat. One of the captains of Mr. Morry's original rust buckets was killed in a ruckus with a family of Laotians. It was only half a year later, when I made an attempt to recover what was left of this man's body, that I heard the quarrel leading to his violent end issued from a disagreement over two small pigs. How bizarre is that? Two black potbellied stouts. His name was Andries and he was a Dutchman. He thought of himself as getting the raw end of that deal, so he came on shore and beat the local village chief with a club. This came as no surprise to me as I had heard of the fellow being a rough and ready, two-fisted kind of a captain. One who had served in the Dutch Navy during the 1950s. But in this case, his bombastic nature was his downfall. After he had beaten the old fellow to near unconsciousness, one of the chief's sons shot the hot-headed Netherlander in the chest. Afterwards the entire village disappeared into the jungle, fearful of the reprisals they were sure would follow. Meanwhile, the freighter Andries had commanded left also in a frenzied panic, its controls being taken over by the ship's young first mate. As though embarrassed by the incident, nobody, not even his employer, seemed interested in locating his remains. Then I arrived in Laos and took charge of his ship along with the company's other sailing craft.

I couldn't let Andries' bones lay forgotten, so at the first opportunity, I got together a search party and went looking for what remained of him. Indeed though, so much time had passed that all I could find was his skull and one of his hands, all gone to bone. Tall grass had grown over these ghastly fragments of the man, hiding them well. What's more, there was grass growing out of the skull's mouth and eye sockets. Grass covered the skeletal hand's joints like a mat of green hair and adding an odd touch of macabre beauty, a purple orchid blossom was sprouting from the crown of the unfortunate Dutchman's head. Right away, I got in touch with the man's family in Amsterdam and shipped his remains to them. They replied to me with relief and gratitude. Now they knew what had become of their testy, but beloved Andries.

As for the village where he had met his ruin, it was now a deserted wreak. The huts were all gaping and fallen in. The inhabitants had all fled elsewhere. Blind fear had scattered them to the depths of the palm and vine shrouded jungle from which they would never return. As for the pigs, I never did find out what their fate had been. I have no doubt though that they wound up as the main course on someone's table. And I had other concerns. Now I had a trading company to be the middle man for and I applied myself to my new position with alacrity.

Mr. Morry's representative, an American named Billy Keopfer, had his headquarters deep in the jungle near the Nam Song River. He liked to live very remotely and you had to walk across several unwieldy bamboo bridges in order to get to his mansion which resembled a classic southern townhouse, white pillars and all. But for me, that was all part of the adventure. After I met the man, who was a rotund blond fellow who always wore white and looked like a weathered version of Colonel Sanders, we became fast friends. I was fascinated by

187

his antique gun collection and his cultivating the customs and habits of his birthplace in the deep south. 'You can take a man out of Virginia, but you can't take Virginia out of the man,' he told me as he poured me a glass of smooth Southern Comfort whiskey. Together we drank to our mutual American homeland and then got down to business. I would be overseeing the purchase of silks, spices, and other goods from the Laotians. It would also be my job to make sure that all of these trade items were shipped to America where they would be sold in stores. As I put myself to these tasks, my most thrilling and strange adventures began. Oh, the places I saw and the people I met would fill a book. I made the acquaintance of a Buddhist priest who got a ride on one of my ships and blessed the captain and whole crew with a prayer that must have had angel's wings.

From then on, the boat never sank nor hit a snag and everyone on board remained in good health, even while tropical diseases were raging all around them. During a trip to pick up a load of bamboo furniture from a village in the mountains, I went off trail and discovered a cave full of golden Buddha statues. I was able to work out a deal with the Laos Government and make a real profit from that find.

There was the time when one of my dock loading crews was attacked by a rogue elephant. It appears the huge behemoth ate too many fermented papayas and went berserk drunk. I've found ancient relics in rice paddies and temples thousands of years old deep in the jungle. I've fought bandits and tigers by hand. But my greatest adventure happened two years after I had signed on with Morry's Exotics.

I happened to be negotiating a business deal with a spice merchant in the city of Hôngsa when a storm broke out. It was a terrific monsoon, rain was coming down in buckets, so the fellow offered me and my men overnight shelter at his roomy villa. That night as the rain pounded and lightening lit up the nearby foliage, my host took me through his whole house where I discovered wonder after wonder. Every room had a marvel. I saw ivory statues and tapestries woven with gold and silver threads. But in the room that was set aside for me, was the greatest treasure and mystery of them all. Across from my silk draped bed was a large heavily lacquered cabinet. My host explained that it was imported from some unknown village in Mongolia. That started my curiosity going and I asked him more questions about the cryptic piece of furniture, but he was unwilling or unable to give me more information concerning its history.

Over supper I talked with my merchant friend about him supplying me with thousands of dollars' worth of basil. It didn't take us long to work out a deal, since he had several spice farms and was eager for the American money I had to offer. After signing a contract, he and I talked way into the night about his past. As it turned out, he had been a farmer in Cambodia before Pol Pot took over and after the Khmer Rouge seized control had made huge sums of money doing spy work for Pol Pot's enemies. When that notorious tyrant was finally overthrown, he had taken this money and established his first spice farm in Cambodia. Many more were to follow, both in Laos and in his native land. Yes, Ching Chok, whose name means "fox" in his native tongue, is a fox indeed.

That stormy night in his lavish domain, I tried to sleep but the violence of the monsoon and my own curiosity about the fascinating lacquered cabinet would not let me rest my eyes for long. I turned on the lamp on my bed table and walked over to it. In my hand was a high-powered flashlight so I could look in every nook and cranny. As I opened its door, which was red with a gold leaf and flower design, I noticed that it was bigger inside than it had first appeared. On the lowest part of it were drawers with golden knobs, while above these was a shelf. I pulled out each drawer and found nothing in any of them.

189

There was nothing on the shelf either, only stark blackness. I beamed the light of my flashlight to the back and saw only smooth wood, like mahogany. For no reason other than plain curiosity, I reached my hand to the back and, I swear to God, it went right through it. I felt open air and a cool breeze on my skin. With puzzlement rather then shock, I quickly pulled my hand out of the curious crack in space and time and back into the cabinet.

Being an adventurer, I was not going to let an opportunity to get to the bottom of the strange phenomena pass me by. Did my hand really go all the way through the wood or was I dreaming? The only way I could find out for sure was to do a little on the spot exploring. I put my tan-colored leisure suit back on with my shoes. I also put my pistol in my pocket and with flashlight in hand, prepared to find out what if anything was actually in back of that tall cabinet.

I climbed up on the shelf and it bore my weight. I was able to get completely on top of it even though I am over six feet tall. My curiosity and drive as an explorer overcoming my fears, I reached out my hand to the cabinet's back. Again it went completely through. With a sudden leap, I left the shelf and landed on some grassy ground. After quickly recovering my bearings, I stood up and looked around. I was in a forest but nothing like the one surrounding Ching Chok's house. Truly, it more resembled the sort of rocks and flora you would find in the countryside of America's Pacific Northwest. All around me were basalt cliffs and volcanic boulders emerging from the ground. These huge stones were covered with moss and lichens as were the trunks of the abundant pine, oak, and maple trees. To add to the foreignness of the landscape, it was broad daylight and no rain was in sight. In the world on the other side of the cabinet, it was past midnight and raining in torrents.

Cautious, and understandably puzzled, I made my way over a

carpet of pine needles and cushiony moss. In the trees birds called, but they were sparrows, robins, and goldfinches, not the parrots nor jacana water wading fowl I had gotten used to seeing ever since I had planted myself in Indochina. All around me, spring seemed to be the air and in every living thing. I heard rustling in a nearby flowering thimbleberry bush and momentarily froze, putting my hand to my pocketed gun as a mindless reflex. A moment later, a doe raised her graceful, large-eared head over the top of the bush and eyed me with cautious, melting brown eyes. Then she was bounding away on her long, slender legs. I laughed to myself, thinking of the deer I had seen in my native Maine and during business trips to the places like Crater Lake in Washington State and Medford, Oregon. In those areas, herds of deer would come fearlessly into towns and parks. Sometimes, raccoons and porcupines would make their appearances as well. I expected some of the latter wild critters to come into my view as well. I rather wanted to see a porcupine.

I never did see one of those walking pincushions during this outlandish excursion. I did, however, see a large beaver waddle out of the woods and then just stand in a flower covered clearing, eyeing me with a boldness and wonder I thought very uncommon. Usually, wild things, when they spy a human, try to get out of there quick. But this little paddle tailed guy just stood in the clearing and he was only three feet away from me. 'Well, hello, little fellow,' I told him as I leaned over and looked into his bright brown eyes. I have always liked animals and missed the kind that are commonly seen in and around my Maine hometown.

Still unfearing, but not eager to make friends, the beaver turned his furry back on me and waddled over to the boulder filled stream that flowed near by. Quicker than a wink, he disappeared into the water. Wanting to take a closer look and see where his dam was, I walked over to the large rolling brook.

At that moment, I heard a strange grating sound. I looked around until I saw what looked like a section of stone that was sliding out of the face of the nearby cliff. It was opening like a doorway. At that moment, it wouldn't have surprised me if a giant with a club and fur cloak had emerged from that peculiar opening. Instead out came a creature that was just as astonishing. It was an enormous gray wolf, bigger than any such animal I had ever seen before. On instinct, my hand went for my gun, but I left it there and soon started to cautiously relax. There was something otherworldly and benign, almost regal, about that wolf that caused me to let my guard down. In his own way, the creature seemed to be smiling as he walked towards me and then sat down on his hunches. Then he caused me to be taken aback by speaking and, even more incredibly, speaking my name.

'Greetings, Tomas, and welcome to the land of Parciful,' he said in a voice that boomed, but carried a tone of friendliness. 'Y-you can talk and you know who I am,' I blurted out, beginning to believe that I must be drunk, dreaming, or both. 'Yes, I can, Tomas, and I know your name as well. Your full name is 'Tomas Gresham', said the wolf in a voice that was resonant and full of authority, but still carried a friendly quality. 'Where am I? This is nothing like anywhere in Laos?' I asked as I removed my cap. The creature seemed so kingly in a strange way that I felt the need to show him proper respect. 'This is the land of Parsiful on the world of Yergo, an entirely different world from Earth,' the wolf continued with as close as any canine could to a benign smile. 'Then I am on another planet,' I ventured, still wondering if all this was real. 'That's about right,' said the lordly wolf. 'And what is your name, Sir?' I inquired. 'Canuck,' said the wolf patiently. 'Okay, Mr. Canuck, I seem to have gotten here by walking through that cabinet over there,' I said although I felt that I was stating the obvious. 'There are many portals, many bridges between your world and mine. That chest is one of several,' explained Canuck.

'Blows me away. This seems so unreal,' I admitted, showing my puzzled mental state. 'I assure you, Tomas, everything you are seeing and experiencing here and now is real. The ground is real, the air is real, the sky is real, and I am real,' 'This is quite the adventure. I could kick myself for thinking to bring everything but a camera,' I admitted while feeling honestly exasperated at myself for the oversight. '*Ha ha.* You will be coming back here again, Tomas. Plenty of time to take pictures on some other day,' replied Canuck in a manner meant to set me at ease. But my feelings of being perplexed were still building. 'How do you know I will be visiting here again?' I asked. 'Because I was the one who brought you here, Tomas. I was the one who made the back of that dresser a portal,' said the wolf in a sudden revelation. 'Why did you bring me here then?' I ventured, more puzzled than before. 'To give you this message and this mission. Captain Tomas Gresham, you are to leave your trading business in Asia and buy a barge on the Columbia River between Washington and Oregon,' explained the great wolf. 'You will make your living hauling goods between those two states. With the turn of the century, you will meet a couple, a man and a woman named Andy and April, and take them to an abandoned cabin on the Columbia's northern shore. In there, they will find a portal to my world in the form of a mirror.'"

At that juncture and on hearing our names mentioned, Andy and I were quite taken aback. Also, Captain Gresham paused in his dialogue as though he wanted that part of his story to have time to really soak into our heads. We didn't say anything, however, but merely nodded at the good Captain, wanting him to continue. He obliged us by enlarging on the words Canuck had supposedly given him.

"'Now you must leave here, Tomas,' the lordly wolf told me, almost with a tone of regret. 'Return to your world through the cabinet and await my further instructions. So that you will believe me, here is a token that our meeting here was real,' after making that announcement, Canuck used his impressive mouth to pick up a silver ring with a strange jewel-like setting. He placed it in my hand and then left. I thanked him and then made my way back through the lacquered cabinet. After waking up the next morning, I really believed I had been dreaming. Then I found the silver ring and knew that the kingly wolf and all had to have been a real otherworldly experience. The ring setting itself is shaped like a wolf's head, but the jewel in it gleams in colors the way no earthly stone could. Depending on which direction you turn it in the light, it will by turns gleam white, then purple, then blue. I later had it analyzed by a chemist and he could not place the jewel as belonging in any known mineral category."

On saying that, Captain Gresham had both Andy and me take a closer look at the ring he was wearing. It did indeed reflect colors the way no gem on Earth usually did. Andy and I gasped in astonishment.

"I believe you," said my beloved. "so when will you take us to this cabin with the entrance to that other world?

"Right now, my friend," said Captain Gresham as he ended his dialogue and took his place at the boat's controls.

Andy and I held fast to our seats as our dogs continued to snooze on blankets in their corner of the boats. As soon as the boat's mighty motor revved up, both of them were awake and ready for anything. We sped along on the waves and before long arrived at the bank near the northern branch of the river. A broken down but still serviceable pier was there waiting for us. After bringing the boat abreast, the two men leaped out and harnessed the Klickitat Queen to the rickety dock, while I climbed out with both dogs. It didn't take them long to find spots onshore for their potty breaks. After both Skippy and

Pepper had finished their business, I peed behind a bush and then rejoined the men. We walked along a sandy path through a grove of pines. I found seashells and interesting rocks along the way. Andy, the dogs, and I continued walking with Captain Gresham in the lead. On the way, we chatted and made remarks about the local animals and scenery. A squirrel darted across our path and then scurried up a tree, from which vantage point it began scolding us heartily. Pepper and Skippy both barked back defiantly to the great amusement of us humans. Frogs sang out a chorus from a nearby gurgling stream. We also snacked as I had brought a large bag of trail mix along. It was just as well that we had something to munch on since it took us more than an hour to reach our destination. The door of a house so old its wood had turned gray and here and there its roof had caved in.

On flimsy wooden steps, we walked up to this door that was rotting off its hinges. As we entered it, a white owl flew past us. This startled the dogs most of all. Both of them began a rousing chorus of barking as the bird flew out the door and up into a nearby birch tree. Dusk was starting to fall over the horizon, so the nocturnal hunter was right in its element. In response to the dimming light around us and already cave-like darkness inside the crumbling building, Captain Gresham produced a flashlight to help us all see our way.

"If an owl's been roosting in here, there's got to be piles of owl pellets," said Andy who was eager to find these regurgitated remains of an owl meal.

These pellets are made up of the parts of the owl's prey that it can't digest, like the fur, bones, and teeth of some small mouse. He began to look around in hopes of finding some. I, however, was the one who found a trophy worth claiming. As we walked through what used to be the kitchen into the wreck of a parlor, I glanced by a staircase and found a cloth doll dressed as a Yakama Indian lady. Although she was in bad shape from years of neglect and gathering dust and cobwebs, the bead work on her leather dress was still impressive.

"May I have that doll?" I asked Capt. Gresham on impulse.

"You may, April," he answered as he paused for a moment to look at the cloth munchkin himself. Her braids appeared to be made of real black hair and were entwined with feathers.

"But doesn't that doll belong to someone? Possibly the descendant of whoever owns this old house," I asked, suddenly having second thoughts.

"That would be me," said Capt. Gresham in a soft, encouraging voice. "And I say you can have it."

Happy to have another doll to add to my collection, I took hold of it and followed him, Andy, and the dogs into a mouldering bedroom. This room had its own unique features. In its center was a bed crowned by a canopy and shrouded by a white bedspread made gray with ages of dust and cobwebs. On the wall to the side of it was a large hexagonal window which let in no light, only a view of the nearby shadow- haunted forest. But most intriguing of all was a tall, long, tarnished mirror that stood in the corner opposite the odd-shaped window. It was cracked in places, a testimony to the futility of long past days of vanity. Andy thought he saw some owl pellets in the room's small closet and went to see if there were any. In a few minutes, he returned to our party, his face registering disappointment. But he would keep looking.

At that juncture, the bold captain led all of us over to the mirror.

"This is another portal to the land of Parciful," he said motioning towards it.
"Really? Through that mirror?" I asked, remembering all of

the stories I had read about the possibility of such doorways into other worlds.

Not the least of these was *Alice Through The Looking Glass,* the author Lewis Carroll's whimsical and enchanting sequel to his epic *Alice In Wonderland.* In my library, I have original copies of both classic books, each of which were signed by Carroll himself. Indeed, I felt like a latter-day adult version of the young lady in those allegorical children's tales as I watched our host stick his hand into the surface of the looking glass before him and pull it out again as easily as if it had been a pool of clear water. Andy's light-brown eyes widened with boyish wonder behind his trim spectacles.

"Yes, April, through this mirror," said Captain Gresham with calm earnestness. I could see that his hand had been unharmed by its temporarily being slipped into the reflective glass.

"So, will you follow me in and find out your life's true course? Canuck is back in there and he has all of the answers you two are seeking," he added as he turned to us with an inviting smile. As if to remind him that they too didn't plan on being left out of any adventure, Pepper and Skippy barked for recognition.

"Oh yes," said Gresham with a laugh as he leaned down and petted the canines' furry heads. "You two dogs are a most welcome part of this journey and won't be left out, I promise. Then he stood up.

"Follow me!" the tall fellow announced in a way that was both commanding and inviting. Then he dove headfirst into the long bedroom mirror. It appeared to swallow him up, lanky legs and all.

"Well, April, here we go!" exclaimed Andy as he grabbed hold of my hand and hurried to perform his own mirror jump.

"Land of Parciful, here we come!" I said as he pulled me into the portal with him. I had both dogs under my arms.

As I went through the mirror, I heard a loud *whooosh* sound and felt like I was flying through an energy field. Both Pepper and Skippy were squirming nervously. A second later, my feet were on a sort of solid ground. I was too stunned to take in everything that I saw, felt, and heard at the moment, but I managed to put the dogs down and see that Andy and Captain Gresham were right beside me. I began to feel more oriented and secure, especially when the two men started speaking to me.

"Whew!" exclaimed my boyfriend as he put his strong arm around my shoulder. "That was quite a trip. I guess we're in Parciful now?"

"We are, my friends. Just stay with me because otherwise you could get lost in a hurry," cautioned our companion as he led us across a field that looked like a farm field in the rural Columbia Gorge.

The forest and deer were the same as was the blue sky in which billows of clouds sped by like white airships on the wind. But here the air seemed fresher and the whole terrain was bathed in an atmosphere of peace and order that was lacking anywhere on Earth. The whole landscape also seemed free of pollution of any form.

We walked along a simple grassy path that led us past clear water brooks, groves of pine and birch trees where birds nested and squirrels perched, and up a hill studded with pitted, huge, gray basaltic boulders. All in all, the terrain resembled that of Goldendale's woodsy Ekone Park, but this place seemed

lovelier and purer. Everywhere wild flowers, including dai-
sies and poppies, bloomed in clumps. It was like spring in
the Klickitat, only more so. True to their curious dog natures,
Pepper and Skippy ran along sniffing everything in reach. I let
my little girl be off her leash, because I sensed by some instinct
that nothing in this world could hurt her. Then too, she and her
canine boy pal seemed to want to stay close by us humans. It
was as though they felt that if they wondered off by themselves
they might miss something.

After reaching the top of the hill, we came down on the other
side and found a camp situated in a clearing. This camp was
made of teepees which were unlike any found in a traditional
Native American Village of the days before skyscrapers and
motor cars. For one thing, these structures, which appeared
to be covered by deer skin, were all solid bright colors. Reds,
blues, and golden-yellows dominated. What's more, these teepees were studded all over with intricate designs in bead work
unlike any I had ever seen before. Incredibly, none of them
had or seemed to need to have, poles to prop them up. They
appeared to be held in place by some force that could only exist
in this other- worldly realm. All around these teepees were
people, moving in and out and busying themselves with chores.
They all wore feathers in their hair and beaded, fringed clothing made of soft animal hide. Seen from a distance, I guessed
them all to be very like our earthly Native American folk. But
when my party and I got closer to them, I saw that a few of
these villagers actually had blue eyes and blond braids. Some
even had African features and hair. Even more surprisingly,
there were a handful that weren't human. I saw one with the
head and paws of a beaver, while another was, no mistaking it,
a fox that walked upright. For some reason, I thought of the
Power Animals of Native American folklore. Every person
is said to have some animal spirit as their guide and mentor,
whether they happen to be aware of it or not. As I gazed with
wonder on these animal-like beings, I thought to myself that

maybe this magical realm might be where such legends had their origins. As we continued our approach, these villagers came on the alert, though not in any threatening manner. I reckoned it was because they were familiar with our captain host. Indeed, he was as at ease in this alien environment as he would have been in a place that was like a "second home" to him.

"This, friends, is where Canuck has made his camp this season. You see, he travels around a lot because he is no ordinary wolf," explained Captain Gresham as he waved at the people near the strange teepees.

They all waved back and smiled. When we were finally in the village itself, the whole view was even more unearthly. For one thing, there were horses that looked like the familiar Palomino "painted ponies". But, when I looked at their feet, I saw that they had toes, like the prehistoric Eohippus, rather than hooves. And the dogs could all talk and walk on their hind legs. But they still remained close to their canine nature. When these latter creatures met Pepper and Skippy, they began talking with them dog style and got quite a barking conversation going. At the same time, Captain Gresham had started talking with a man with a lot of feathers in his dark braids who appeared to be those "people's" chief or one of their tribal elders. The language they spoke was different from any Native American tongue on Earth, but seemed to carry elements of the Yakama dialect.

After Captain Gresham and the fellow had talked for a spell, he introduced him to us.

"April and Andy, meet Red Feather, he's the Chief here and is very close to our wolf friend, Canuck," said the captain as each one of us shook hands with the man whom I noticed had some interesting tattoos on his wrists. They looked like wolfs, they did.

"Welcome, to Parciful, April and Andy," said the tribal leader who actually shared authority with several village Elders with Canuck reigning above them all. "Sit down by the central village fire and Canuck will be with you in a short while."

With that invitation, Chief Red Feather led my party, which now included Pepper and Skippy who had left their new dog friends, to some seats made of tree branches and leather. There were eight of them that formed a circle around a blazing fire enclosed in a pit made of stones. In the pit was a deer turning on a spit. Looking at it, made me feel hungry and I hoped that I would be given a chance to partake of it at some point. Red Feather left us and went to a teepee that was bright red and adorned with pictures and bead work that were golden-yellow and shaped like wolf's heads.

Thankfully, at that point, I was distracted from my hungry longing by the appearance of Canuck himself. He emerged from the red teepee as some of the villagers pounded drums and danced in his honor.

"Greetings, friends. Welcome to Yergo, in particular the Land of Parciful where you are now," he announced in a way that was regal, but still friendly and inviting.

"Greetings and honor to you, Lord Canuck. It's been a while, but I feel that I'm back home again. And here are the two people you wanted me to bring you, along with their dogs," said Captain Gresham as he removed his cap and tipped his head to the regal wolf with great respect.

"Hello, Lord Canuck. This place sure is a wonder," remarked Andy as he bowed his own head to the imposing wolf.

"I'm honored to meet you, sir," I said with sincere awe. Pepper and Skippy weren't so formal. Before I could stop them, they had broken away from me and Andy and ran to the friendly wolf, barking and squirming like puppies. He smiled, in his own wolf way, and scampered playfully with them, his broad gray tail wagging. After a few minutes of canine cavorting, the three of them settled down and our dogs returned to us. Canuck sat on his haunches near me and my male companions and spoke in a grand, but hospitable way.

"It is good to see you again, Tomas, and good to see that aside from a slight calcification of your heart, you are in perfect health," said the great wolf to our friend who was holding his yachting cap in both hands and smiling with humble gratitude.

"I'm honored to be here in your kingdom again, Canuck. And while it's true that my heart isn't in the best shape, I feel that everything else is. In fact, I never felt better," replied the captain.

"Such is the way of life on Earth. As long as you live there, you will always have a few health issues. Some get them when they are older, some get them a lot sooner. You, Andy and April, have problems of your own concerning health," explained the large wolf with a note of empathy in his deep voice.

"Yes, we know," I said a little sadly thinking of my own recent crisis with cancer.

"You will have to take both a hormone blocker pill and an antibody pill while you are living on the Earth. But have no fear, April. All will go well for you," said the mighty gray wolf.

That revelation wasn't anything I hadn't heard before, mostly from doctors. I tried to take it as good news, however, and pulled myself up tall and smiled bravely.
"Now April, you needn't despair because here is an herb called 'ruddy root' which will do magic in your body to both take away the side effects of the infusions you were taking and

ensure that the side effects of the new medications will be so slight you'll hardly notice them at all. Chief Red Feathers, bring her the ruddy root pills," Canuck commanded. In response, the man in the fringed, beige leather suit placed a glass bottle full of the red capsules in my hands.

"To your health, dear sister. May the Great Spirit bless you with a long, cancer-free life," said Red Feathers.

"Take one every day, April," Canuck added. "And rest assured, you are completely cured of the cancer, no matter what some may say."

I thanked him and Red Feathers and held the bottle like it was my own personal elixir of life. I turned to Andy and grinned, no longer feeling that my victory over cancer was a Pyrrhic one.

"This same herb will help with your diabetes, Andy. However, you will still have to be careful of your blood sugar as long as you make your home anyplace on Earth," added the gray wolf to my beloved who had been needing a health victory of his own.

But Canuck had even better news to share.

"April and Andy, I must bid you go to return to your world where you and your dogs will spend two more years. During this time you will both achieve much with writing books. Together, you will also open a restaurant that serves delicious home style meals in a country atmosphere. Then at the end of those two years, dear little Pepper will be nearing the end of her life. So you will return here to Parciful with her and she will become young again. Both of you and Skippy will be young again too and, while you won't live forever, all four of you will live longer than humans and canines commonly do on the planet of your origin. What's more, you, Andy and April, will open a country inn in this land and will be acclaimed authors as well. As an added joy, you will marry and have several children. All of your dreams and wishes will come true, April, because managing time here won't be the problem it was for you while you were living on Earth. Your problems with time and organization stem from your autism which you will be free of forever. That disability has been messing with your life since day one. Neither you nor Andy will have weight problems because, in this blessed realm, a person's body converts what they eat to energy and not to fat storage. As for you, faithful Tomas, you will return here and join my tribe at the end of those same two years."

After he had given me, Andy, and the captain this good news of our joyful future, Canuck invited our whole party to enjoy a little time in Parciful. When evening came, we ate the venison and drank mead while talking with the great wolf's friends and courtiers. All of them were fascinating and had exciting adventures to relate. One was from the fox being who had recently done a battle with a tribe of hostile giants. We were also joined by my own special friend, Billy Brave Salmon.

"I had to come and give you a blessing for good medicine during your visit here," said Billy who was happy to see me, Andy, and our dogs. We introduced him to our friend, Captain Gresham.

"Is this your first visit here, Tomas?" Billy asked him.

"No, I've met Canuck here more than once. How often do you come here?" the captain was eager to know.

"I come to this world often to see Canuck. You see, he's no ordinary wolf," said Billy with deep feeling as he took a piece of deer meat from the serving platter.
"In truth, he is very extraordinary," agreed Capt. Gresham as he

sipped a clay drinking cup brimful of mead. The two men then began a lively discussion about their meetings with Canuck, in Parciful and elsewhere.

During the meal, men dressed in animal skins and feathers did lively dances to the beat of the resounding drums and tinkling rattles. Incense and smudge sticks made a tantalizing aroma, along with the wood smoke, food, and nearby pine trees. All around us whirred the wind that made a special music of its own. Everyone and everything seemed to be full of magic in a close to nature sort of way.

When the supper and talk were done, it was very dark and unfamiliar constellations had begun to sparkle in the sky. The three of us then decided that it was time to return to the world which was to remain our home for the span of two more years. Before leaving his encampment, all of us, including the dogs, took turns hugging Canuck. When we finally left, he was sad but encouraging.

"All of you will return when the Great Spirit says its time," he reassured us as we walked away.

With the captain to guide our way, the rest of us made it back to a mirror that stood in a clearing. It was half-covered with the branches of trees and would have been hard for me to find had I been alone. To Captain Gresham, however, this was all a routine he was so familiar with he could have gone through it blindfolded.

"Follow me, friends," he announced as he first stuck his hand through the magical looking glass. In a moment, the rest of him had disappeared through it. Right behind him, Andy pulled me and the dogs in with him.

Once again, there was the same *whooosh* and the feeling of

going through an energy vortex. An instant later, all five of us were back in the spider-plagued bedroom. Pepper felt a bit bewildered and barked. I picked her up and cuddled her protectively.

"Was that real?" asked Andy as he leaned down to console Skippy.

"Or were we dreaming?" I asked, half-believing, half-stunned.

"Oh it was real alright," laughed Captain Gresham as he flashed his many-colored ring at us.

"And to prove it, Andy," here are some souvenirs.

This was said by a large white owl who came flying out of the mirror and placed three owl pellets in my boyfriend's hand.

"You might as well take them, good human, they are of no use to me whatsoever," explained the venerable fowl as he sped back through the looking glass portal, making believers of us all.

THE END
BUT NOT OF MY LIFE!

www.ingramcontent.com/pod-product-compliance
Lightning Source LLC
Chambersburg PA
CBHW060922250626
47159CB00008B/3126

* 9 780999 385884 *